ONCE HE TAKES

(A Claire King FBI Suspense Thriller —Book 3)

Molly Black

Molly Black

Bestselling author Molly Black is author of the MAYA GRAY FBI suspense thriller series, comprising nine books (and counting); of the RYLIE WOLF FBI suspense thriller series, comprising six books; of the TAYLOR SAGE FBI suspense thriller series, comprising eight books; of the KATIE WINTER FBI suspense thriller series, comprising eleven books (and counting); of the RUBY HUNTER FBI suspense thriller series, comprising five books (and counting); of the CAITLIN DARE FBI suspense thriller series, comprising five books (and counting); of the REESE LINK mystery series, comprising five books (and counting); of the CLAIRE KING FBI suspense thriller series, comprising five books (and counting); and of the GRACE FORD FBI suspense thriller series, comprising five books (and counting).

An avid reader and lifelong fan of the mystery and thriller genres, Molly loves to hear from you, so please feel free to visit www.mollyblackauthor.com to learn more and stay in touch.

ISBN: 978-1-0943-7929-6

BOOKS BY MOLLY BLACK

GRACE FORD MYSTERY SERIES
NEARLY MINE (Book #1)
NEARLY SAFE (Book #2)
NEARLY FREE (Book #3)
NEARLY GONE (Book #4)
NEARLY HIS (Book #5)

CLAIRE KING MYSTERY SERIES
ONCE HE SEES (Book #1)
ONCE HE LONGS (Book #2)
ONCE HE TAKES (Book #3)
ONCE HE FEELS (Book #4)
ONCE HE KNOWS (Book #5)

MAYA GRAY MYSTERY SERIES
GIRL ONE: MURDER (Book #1)
GIRL TWO: TAKEN (Book #2)
GIRL THREE: TRAPPED (Book #3)
GIRL FOUR: LURED (Book #4)
GIRL FIVE: BOUND (Book #5)
GIRL SIX: FORSAKEN (Book #6)
GIRL SEVEN: CRAVED (Book #7)
GIRL EIGHT: HUNTED (Book #8)
GIRL NINE: GONE (Book #9)

RYLIE WOLF FBI SUSPENSE THRILLER
FOUND YOU (Book #1)
CAUGHT YOU (Book #2)
SEE YOU (Book #3)
WANT YOU (Book #4)
TAKE YOU (Book #5)
DARE YOU (Book #6)

TAYLOR SAGE FBI SUSPENSE THRILLER

DON'T LOOK (Book #1)
DON'T BREATHE (Book #2)
DON'T RUN (Book #3)
DON'T FLINCH (Book #4)
DON'T REMEMBER (Book #5)
DON'T TELL (Book #6)

KATIE WINTER FBI SUSPENSE THRILLER

SAVE ME (Book #1)
REACH ME (Book #2)
HIDE ME (Book #3)
BELIEVE ME (Book #4)
HELP ME (Book #5)
FORGET ME (Book #6)
HOLD ME (Book #7)
PROTECT ME (Book #8)
REMEMBER ME (Book #9)
CATCH ME (Book #10)
WATCH ME (Book #11)

RUBY HUNTER FBI SUSPENSE THRILLER

IF I RUN (Book #1)
IF I TELL (Book #2)
IF I LIVE (Book #3)
IF I FORGET (Book #4)
IF I RETURN (Book #5)

CAITLIN DARE FBI SUSPENSE THRILLER

COME GET ME (Book #1)
COME FIND ME (Book #2)
COME TAKE ME (Book #3)
COME CATCH ME (Book #4)
COME SAVE ME (Book #5)

REESE LINK MYSTERY

BEYOND REASON (Book #1)
BEYOND REACH (Book #2)
BEYOND REPAIR (Book #3)
BEYOND DOUBT (Book #4)

BEYOND NORMAL (Book #5)

PROLOGUE

Darkness and cold engulfed him. Those were the first two things that forced their way into his mind. Then there was pain.

No, more discomfort than pain. There were other sensations too that were trying to make themselves known to his foggy brain. Jostling for attention.

There was a noise. Familiar, but he couldn't work out what it was, what it meant, and how it related to him. His nose sucked in cold air, and that brought with it more information. More information, but still no answers. The smell was familiar, but again its source remained just out of reach of his grasping mind.

There was something else though. Something that was causing his heart to race and his mind to veer towards panic.

He couldn't move.

The feeling that he was paralyzed took over everything else, overwhelming him, and pushing every other thought from his panicking brain. The more he fought against the paralysis, the louder the noise became until it filled his ears.

He screamed, suddenly aware he could use his voice, that his lungs were not just there to suck in that familiar smelling cold air. He screamed again, if anything to try and get a hold of reality, and to block out that noise.

That ringing, clanking noise.

Suddenly his eyes sprang open.

The darkness was replaced by a dusty dimness. Slowly, shapes morphed, and his world came into focus, made up of different shades of gray. His eyes darted around his surroundings. Gathering yet more information. And bringing back answers.

All of which only added to the rising panic that was starting to consume him.

He was not paralyzed. He was chained to a radiator. Handcuffs bound his wrists, a thick metal chain looped through them and then wound around the large, cast iron struts of the radiator. The noise that had assaulted his ears and confused him in his initial wakening moments was that of the chain clanking against the ribs of the radiator as he tried to move his arms.

As if to confirm his discovery he shook his hands, the metallic clanking ringing out in reply, mocking him. He swung his head to the left and the right, trying to make out where he was, and why it looked so familiar.

The smell that had teased him was simply that of concrete, oil, and dust. That, added to the gray shapes, the industrial radiator, and the cold dusty floor on which he sat, suddenly all clicked together, like a Chinese puzzle he'd had as a child.

He was in a basement. More than that, he was in his own basement.

Moments of his life flashed through his mind. Happy times. Also the things he wished he had done differently. Things he now so dearly wished he would get a chance to do again.

Faces swam in front of his eyes. Those of people he had loved. Who had even loved him. Faces he so desperately wanted to gaze upon again, to touch. To kiss.

Faces he suddenly doubted he would ever see again.

He tried to get on his knees, but the shortness of the chain made that impossible, forcing him to remain in a crouch that was making his lower back begin to sing in agony.

Then another question forced its way into the front of his mind. Demanded an answer. It was perhaps the most relevant question of all, apart from how he was going to get away, that hadn't even occurred to him yet.

How did he get there?

He tried to remember, to go back to a time before he had emerged from the dark, soupy fog just minutes before.

And it was then that he heard the footsteps.

There was the sound of a key in a lock, then part of the gray wall to his left disappeared, replaced by a rectangle of light. A figure was silhouetted in the middle of it.

Then the rectangle disappeared once more as the door was slammed shut and the figure strode towards him, almost running in his desperation to get to him.

The man chained to the radiator cowered, forcing himself closer to the cold metal. A minute ago he would have welcomed any intrusion, any fellow human. But he knew that this particular fellow human had not come to help him. He had not come to loosen his chains and set him free.

The figure thrust a plastic bottle at him, forcing it into his cold, numb hands.

“Drink it!” the voice said, the words sounding like they were being squeezed from between clenched teeth and taut jaws.

The man stared with wild eyes at the man towering above him, then at the bottle in his hands.

“DRINK IT!” the man shrieked. “DRINK IT!”

His hands shaking, his eyes darted from the face just inches from his own to the bottle gripped in his shaking hands.

Slowly, his fingers unscrewed the lid, his movements clumsy. Then with one last look at the face hovering above him he closed his eyes and put the bottle to his dry lips.

CHAPTER ONE

Agent Claire King sat at her desk, her laptop open in front of her. It should have felt familiar. Safe. Instead, she felt like she was standing on the edge of a cliff. The more she thought about it, and what she was about to do, that cliff deepened until it became an abyss. But she had made up her mind. She had been pushing it back into the depths, running from it for far too long. It was time to face those demons.

She stepped out and launched herself into the abyss.

Claire had been twelve years old when her mom had been killed. Too young to understand what had happened, but exactly the right age for it to have scarred her. Her young, still forming mind had been traumatized by the events. Not just the sudden hole left by the most important person in her life, but by the reactions of those who remained.

Her father had been a distant enough figure before, but with her mom in her life, that distance had not seemed to matter. When her mom was no longer there, instead of closing that distance, her father had increased it. He disappeared into his own grief, wallowed in it. He drank in hopes of abating it, but instead only fueled it.

The distance between father and daughter grew and grew. It quickly became far too great for Claire's adolescent mind to traverse. He made it very clear that there had only been one female in his life, and she had been ripped from him. He had no time for another one, especially one that was just a burden.

Claire had often wondered if the fact that she looked like her mother - dark hair, dark eyes, eyebrows that gave her a studious, serious, even stern look - reminded her father of his dead wife too much. That he could not cope with seeing a reminder of what he had lost, every day, right there in the home they had shared together.

But over the years, when she had thought about it, she had decided that was just a case of her trying to find excuses for her dad's behavior. He was a weak man, a selfish man, and what had happened had destroyed any semblance of desire to be anything else, and certainly any desire to be a father for his daughter.

Claire had spent years trying to understand her father's grief and distant behavior, which had resulted in neglecting her own emotions.

She had buried the pain deep down, refusing to acknowledge it, trying, and almost succeeding in convincing herself that she was okay. But as she grew older, that pain had festered and grown, and she found herself unable to form real connections with anyone. Relationships had come and gone, but none had ever felt truly fulfilling.

So it was as much for herself that she had decided to go back to that dark time twenty years ago, as it was for her father or her mother. Only by finding out exactly what had happened, by laying that ghost to rest, was she really going to be able to go forward with her life, no matter what she tried to convince herself was the truth.

Sporadic texts from her father, even more sporadic voice messages, had urged her to use her connections within the FBI (never her own skills and abilities, she always noted) to find the person who had killed his wife.

That was another reason Claire had delayed: the desire to keep those two aspects of her life distinct and separate. But she realized that was no excuse.

Her fingers flew over the laptop keyboard, the details – sparse though they were – of her mother's case appearing on the screen in front of her. When she had entered everything she knew and had written the request for any further information, her finger hovered over the return button.

She closed her eyes, took a deep breath, and hit return, sending the email.

If she had thought the process would make her feel better, that the fact she had made the decision would ease the burden, she could not have been further from the truth.

Anxiety surged up from the pit of her stomach, almost overwhelming her. She quietly closed the laptop and did the same with her eyes, breathing deeply in an attempt to calm her racing heart.

"Sleeping on the job?"

She opened her eyes to see Wilson's large frame beside her, his rugged, not quite handsome face framed by his short black hair set in a half smile.

"Much as I know you would love to have caught me sleeping, Wilson, I was thinking," Claire replied, forcing a smile. "You should try it occasionally." This time the smile was genuine.

"Touché," Wilson said, sitting down in the chair beside her desk, leaning back, and crossing his arms. "Nice hair by the way."

Claire instinctively ran her hand through the short dark bob. She'd had long hair for as long as she could grow it, but in that horrific incident in Patrick and Patricia Moynahan's house, when she had fought with Grant Holt in that terrible burning room, her hair had been singed.

The first thing she did when she returned home was get her hair cut. It was still a shock every time she looked in the mirror. Every time she caught a glimpse of her reflection in a glass door, or on a piece of shiny metal, she would do a double-take.

But it also felt right. Like a snake who had discarded its old skin in order to grow. That was what she needed to do. Shed her old self, or at least part of it, in order to grow. Cutting her hair and sending that email were two halves of that circle.

"Hmmm," she said, "I just don't know how long it will take me to not think there's someone else staring back at me when I look in the mirror."

"No, trust me," Wilson said, "it looks nice. It suits you."

"You never fail to surprise me Wilson, with your talents. Who'd have thought I'd be adding women's fashion and style to your ever-expanding repertoire!"

"It's true, there are many strings to my bow. You haven't seen half of them yet, believe me."

She watched as he opened his laptop and punched in his password. She liked the way he was a contradiction in almost everything he did. Despite being stocky, tall, and muscular, his movements were smooth and considered, his touch gentle. He was well-read too, and she had discovered he would rather talk about literature than the football game over the weekend. Though he was equally knowledgeable of both.

She had worked with him for only three months and was realizing that the more she found out about him, the more there was *to* find out. She also realized that she was eager to discover as much as she could about him. After losing her last partner, Tyler, she thought the relationship they had enjoyed would never be replicated.

It was still early days, but she was getting more and more convinced that if anyone could replicate it, then it was the man sitting next to her.

"The Chief said there have been developments on the Artist," he said swinging his chair around to face her.

The mention of that name sent a chill through her. The scars and bruises she carried from what had happened to her mother were old. The ones she wore from the Artist were still very fresh. The case had almost killed her. It *had* killed Tyler. She had chased him across the

United States, even had him in her grasp, only for him to slip through her fingers, albeit with a bomb that could – should – have killed him.

"There has been. Of sorts," she said.

"From that footage of him sending you the card?" Wilson said, hope etched into his face.

A postcard that had been sent to Claire, a card that forensics had said had a seventy five percent chance of being written by the Artist, had been tracked down to a small town right there in Illinois. They had managed to find footage that showed a man that could be him delivering it.

"No," Claire couldn't hide the disappointment in her voice. "While we were in California, they pored over every second of tape…" She shook her head. "Nothing. It's a dead end, apart from confirming my thoughts that he did not die in that boat. But, we do have something."

She opened her laptop again and found the relevant email.

"We may have a sighting." She shrugged. "It may be nothing but it's all we have."

"Do you want me to follow up on it?" Wilson asked, obviously disappointed the development wasn't more significant.

"No, don't worry. At this stage I'm just gonna send an information request to the local precinct to look into it and keep me posted."

She opened a new message, typed out exactly that, and sent it, the process making her feel a whole lot better than the last email she had sent, only a few minutes before.

She was just in the process of standing up and asking Wilson if he wanted a coffee, when her phone rang.

She saw the name on the display and picked it up.

"Chief," she said, her eyes on Wilson who had stopped what he was doing and had turned towards his partner.

She listened to the Chief. It was short and to the point as he always was, but there was an edge to his voice, even an air of mystery. Then she did stand up.

"There's a new case. A bad one by the sound of it. Something in the Chief's voice makes me think this is going to be a crazy ride. Come on," she said before picking up her notebook and striding down the corridor in the direction of the Chief's office.

CHAPTER TWO

"I've got a new case. Unusual. With some added complications. Just how you like 'em," the Chief said as soon as the two agents entered his office, not bothering to wait for them to sit down.

Claire had expected nothing different. The Chief was someone you respected, but very few if any would say that he was someone they warmed to, or even knew. She assumed he had a life away from the agency, but what it looked like, Claire hadn't the faintest idea. What she *did* know, however, was that he was very good at his job. As the first Black chief in the agency, he had to be.

The man wasted few words, a habit that made him appear blunter than he actually was. He was a busy man and saw little point in needless conversation. That said, he had shown a softer side when Claire had almost been killed on the boat. If she had ever doubted it before, his reaction to Tyler's death and her near death had proved to her just how much he cared for those who worked for him.

She sat down in a chair in front of the Chief's large but tidy desk. Beside her, Wilson took the other chair.

"What are you working on?" he asked before making the question redundant with his following statement. "Whatever it is, clear it. Delegate."

"I followed up on that lead about the Artist," Claire said. "At this stage it's just information request. That could take anywhere from a few days to a month, even if anything does come of it." She kept quiet about the other email she had sent that morning. That wasn't something she wanted to discuss with the Chief. Not yet, and certainly not at this moment.

The Chief nodded.

"Denver," he said as if that explained more than simply a location. "Two victims. Both male. Victim one is a Daniel Walsh. Forty-eight years old. Divorced, a daughter living in Europe. Ex-wife and only child seem to have nothing to do with him. From the little we have been able to ascertain not many people have got much to say about Mr. Walsh, and the little they have is not very complimentary. He was a landlord, rented out a cheap tenement."

"I'm not sure I've ever heard anyone say anything good about landlords," Wilson said.

"That may be true agent, but Walsh even fails to get up to what is, as you say, a pretty low bar when it comes to popularity ratings, but," he raised a finger, looking in turn at both agents in front of him, "that does not mean we give this case any less time and effort, just as we would if it was some Hollywood starlet laying on the slab."

"How was he killed?" Claire asked, her pen hovering over a page in her notebook.

"Good question, agent. We don't know yet. We are waiting for the coroner to get back. They have sent various samples to the lab." He paused. "But it gets better. Victim two. John Doe, as yet unidentified. There was no wallet, no ID on the body. His fingerprints aren't in the system." He slid four manila folders across the desk, two for each agent, one for each victim.

"But he is male, fifty to sixty years old. Again, no obvious cause of death."

Claire picked up the folders, as Wilson spoke up.

"How do we know these are connected?"

"Because both victims were found chained to a radiator in a basement. Different basements, but both belonging to run down tenement blocks," the Chief answered.

"The same tenement block this… Daniel Walsh rented out?" Claire asked, opening the folder labeled John Doe.

"No, unfortunately, or fortunately not."

Claire looked at the pictures of the second unnamed victim. The Chief was right in his estimation of the man's age. He had thick white hair, a bushy mustache, and a weathered face. The photos showed him chained to the radiator, his eyes closed and his head lolling to one side. There were no obvious signs of trauma, but the look on his face suggested that he had suffered greatly before he died.

Claire flicked though the rest of the information but there was very little. She opened the other folder. This was thicker, but still, from a preliminary look, it didn't give a lot to go on.

"Daniel Walsh was found seven days ago. This other man, two days ago. Can't we fast track the results from the lab? Looking at this, they haven't even done a preliminary report on this John Doe," Claire said, her brow creased.

"Do you watch the news agent?" the Chief asked "Parts of Denver have been like a war zone these past two weeks. There's a turf war going on between the city's two main gangs. There were ten shootings last week alone. The coroner is swamped."

Claire remembered seeing the news report a couple of days ago, not realizing at the time it would impact her so directly.

"I need you two on the ground in Denver," the Chief said. "One, to see if you can't hurry the coroner along. But also to see if you can uncover something from the two basements these two men were found in. These aren't two random killings. This took planning. Were they tied up because they knew something the killer wanted to get out of them? Did they die because they wouldn't or couldn't give that information?"

"Or because of what they *did* tell him?" Claire said.

"Correct. Find out why he chained them up first, and you are halfway to solving this case."

"How far apart were the two bodies found?" Wilson asked.

"Less than a mile as the crow flies, in the same part of the city. The same part where Walsh's apartment block is. We aren't talking high-end housing here agents. The people who rented apartments in these blocks - well without wishing to make assumptions, they must have been desperate. These aren't places many people would choose to live."

"Unless you want to hide perhaps," Claire said, just speculating, thinking aloud.

"Maybe, maybe."

"Would I be right in thinking this area is the same one where this turf war is taking place?" Wilson asked.

"You would be totally right in that assumption, agent," the Chief replied.

"You don't think they could be related in any way?" Claire asked.

"I don't *think* they are purely because two white males in their late middle ages don't tend to fit in with the profile of these gangs, but we can't rule anything out. Perhaps they got caught up in it in some other way. We can't rule anything in or out at this stage. We can't even make an educated guess when we don't even know the identity of one of the victims."

Claire closed the folder. Cases always seemed to fall into two categories. Either there was a huge amount of data and information, or the opposite. The task was to first find the right haystack, and then try to find the needle located within it while sifting out the dead ends, false turns, and all the periphery noise in the process.

The other scenario was when they had very little to nothing to go on. Trying to find a lead or someone to concentrate their efforts on was the hardest part.

This case looked like it firmly sat in the second of those categories.

Beside her, Wilson was poring over the scant information on both victims and she could feel the same frustrations coming off him. She found herself thinking once again about the visions. Those freakish episodes that she had started to experience after coming out of that coma.

They had certainly helped to find both Tyrone Conrad and Grant Holt, the killers of six women. They had certainly saved the lives of several more potential victims.

Claire didn't pretend to understand what they were, what they meant, or how and why she was experiencing them. They were frightening, not just because they gave a very real insight into the minds of the killers and the victims, but because they showed how little she knew about what was going on inside her own brain, and what damage that seventeen minutes when she had died had inflicted on it.

They were frightening, but right then she would have paid money to have one, to get an insight or an opening into this case, so at least they knew where to start looking.

But she was starting to think that they were a thing of the past. They belonged to an episode of her life that was gone. That she would just have to rely on her own normal instincts.

The weird thing was, she couldn't decide if that was a good thing or not. Was she prepared to sacrifice her own grasp on reality, her own sanity, in order to solve case after case? She didn't know the answer to that either.

"There's a flight in an hour and a half. You should be on the ground in Denver in less than five hours," the Chief said, bringing her back to the present. "You don't need me to tell you time is of the essence. What's going on at the coroner's is not going to help."

Claire and Wilson stood up, both grasping the folders.

"Good luck, agents," the Chief said, his dark deep eyes going from one to the other before returning to a pile of paperwork on his desk.

Claire followed her partner out of the office.

The adrenaline of the start of the case seemed even more potent this time, with the knowledge that they were not only flying into the middle of a live double- murder investigation, but were flying into what the Chief, who was not known for his hyperbole, had described as a war zone.

CHAPTER THREE

Claire checked her phone as soon as the A320's wheels touched down. There were plenty of messages, but nothing to do with the two bodies that had been found chained to radiators. She had hoped there would be something: that the coroner had come back with something, perhaps the ID for the second victim.

On the plus side, she told herself, there had not been another body found. In a case like this, she knew only too well it would move fast. A detective's job was to not merely keep up with the killer's actions and processes, but to get ahead of them. To do that you needed to understand what drove him or her, what motivated them to do what ninety-nine percent of society would find abhorrent.

Then you could predict what they were likely to do next.

She felt that they were way behind the eight ball in this case. Playing catch up from a standing start. If they weren't able to make progress quickly, they would only get further behind.

She saw her bag on the luggage carousel and hauled it off, pointing to Wilson's which had just emerged from the chute. Together they wheeled their bags out into the arrivals hall, the familiar throng of eager family members crowding around the barriers, craning their necks for the first glimpse of their loved ones.

Claire felt a pang in her chest. She didn't know exactly what it was, some cocktail of regret, remorse, and grief. This was most likely caused by the realization that she didn't have anyone waiting for her arrival, that there had been no one desperate to lay eyes on her for years, and probably wouldn't be for the foreseeable future. If at all.

Nothing had changed, she knew that, but it must have been the contact with her father that had brought all this back into the spotlight.

"The conspiracy theorists are out in force I see," Wilson said, nodding to a group of men off to one side. Claire hadn't noticed them, though now she could tell they were distinct from the regular people you saw at airports.

She knew of course about the theories that circulated about Denver airport. The artwork, the plaques, the gargoyles, and sculptures. The supposed bunkers. She marveled that people had the time to not just search for answers to mysteries, but to actively search out mysteries *to* find the answers to.

But perhaps they were no different, it was just that she had gone even further and had found a job to do it every day of her life.

They climbed into the cab, Wilson letting out a sigh.

"You forget about the altitude, don't you, then it suddenly sneaks up behind you and takes your legs away," Wilson said.

Claire watched the driver put the bags in the trunk, then put her thoughts into words.

"I know some agents like a blank piece of paper at the start of an investigation, so as not to get their thought processes muddied by anyone else. But it seems at the minute we just don't have anything to go after."

Wilson nodded, aware of the driver's eyes studying them in the rear-view mirror. They had gone through the case notes again on the flight, hoping to see something that the Chief had missed but the information they had was flimsy at best.

"Once we know the second victim, then we can start to make connections," he said, his voice low. "I remember you telling me in our first week working together, it was a matter of making triangles. Two data points, be they victims or whatever just create a straight line. Once you have three, then you can start to make triangles. Join the dots."

"You actually listened to what I was saying?" she said smiling. "I have a habit of thinking aloud. Tyler developed the skill of being able to filter out the nonsense. I'd suggest you try to do the same. I'll warn you, sometimes the gospel according to Claire King is not all you maybe think it's cracked up to be."

"Don't put yourself down, Claire. I've learned more in the few weeks I've been working with you than in my previous three years in the agency put together."

She looked at Wilson out of the corner of her eye. He would never have known it, but his kind words – even if he was just massaging her ego – meant the world to her at that moment. The events of the last few weeks, months even, added to by the sudden realization that she was going to have to face her past, had left her emotionally battered.

"Going back to those triangles," Wilson continued, "I admit, I had no idea what you were on about at the time. But I've been thinking about it a lot since. It's a nice way of putting it."

Claire gave him a smile of acknowledgement, then turned to look out the window, not wishing her partner to see the emotion on her face.

The Rocky Mountains stretched in a line in the distance, their summits still topped with snow.

An hour later, they had dropped their bags at the hotel, picked up the keys to their car, and were on the way to the apartment block where the second victim, the John Doe, had been found. Claire watched the streets and buildings becoming more and more run down as they neared their destination. What stores remained open cowered behind metal grills and shutters. Liquor stores and pawn shops had taken over from boutiques and restaurants.

Gangs of men, some young, many in their thirties and forties, hung around on the corners of each block. The whole area had a feeling as if it was waiting for something to happen. And whatever that something was, Claire was pretty sure that it was not going to be good.

The Chief's words about a war zone came back to her.

"There it is," Wilson said, pointing to a cinder-colored block up ahead on their right. Claire guessed it was eight stories high. A rectangular block that sat self-consciously on the corner. The plots on either side of it were fenced-off areas, that maybe once had been earmarked for development, but now just stood vacant, deserted, scrubby vegetation and garbage vying for supremacy.

The smell in the dank foyer was a heady mixture of stale cigarette smoke and urine. The elevator had an out of order sign taped to it that looked like it had been there since before Claire had graduated.

A uniformed officer appeared out of the gloom of the adjacent stairwell, his pressed shirt and shiny leather belt looking out of place in such a setting.

Claire held up her badge.

"Agent King, can you show us where the body was found?"

The policeman, in his early fifties, a belly putting the lower two buttons of his shirt under considerable pressure, paused before replying.

"I could, but I'm guessing that's your shiny vehicle out here," he indicated with his florid head to where Wilson had just parked. "And if you want it to be in working order when you come back out, my time is gonna be better spent watching that than walking you down a flight of stairs."

Claire looked at him and gave a brief nod.

"You may have noticed on your drive over here," the man said, "this isn't the most, shall we say, affluent of areas."

"Yeah, I can't imagine it being featured on many 'Come To Denver' brochures," Wilson said.

The officer nodded and hauled up his pants before making his way slowly to the door that led outside. When he was halfway there, he turned around.

"Down those stairs. You can't miss it. There's only one radiator. If you need anything, you know where I am." He gave both agents a brief but measured look, then continued on his route to the door.

If the smell in the foyer had been unpleasant, that in the stairwell notched it up a couple of levels. The wide stone steps led them down and around, their eyes gradually getting used to the gloom. At the bottom, a short corridor opened out into the basement. Pipework ran around the tops of three of the walls, and two bicycles, chained but without their full complement of wheels, leaned on the wall to their right. The only light was that which managed to squeeze through the gaps of a boarded-up window in the wall in front of them.

Claire got her bearings and realized that it would overlook the street where they had parked. She got a flashlight from her pocket and used it to locate a light switch on the wall, and flicked it on.

There was a buzz, then a naked light bulb hung from the center of the ceiling burst into life. The light, nowhere near bright enough to dispense the gloom, seemed to highlight the darkness of the areas of the room it didn't reach. The corners and the corridor down which they had just walked shrank into darkness.

The wall on their left contained the only other item of note. The radiator that John Doe had been chained to.

Claire walked slowly over to it, getting the photos from the file that had been taken of him before his chains had been cut and his body shipped off to the coroner's.

She orientated it with her own view, pictured the man sitting there, spending the last minutes of his life fastened to the cast iron. She looked around the room, the last place he would have seen, and a shiver went through her.

She reached out to touch the radiator, her fingers on the cold metal before she realized it was a gesture she had grown used to performing in an attempt to summon up a vision. She had done it this time to test the temperature, and that was the only thing she discovered. Fleetingly, she wondered if she would ever have a vision again.

"Cold," she said. "This doesn't strike me as a place where the apartments upstairs are heated, never mind the basement."

She crouched down, her eyes scanning the dark gray metal, the cold, dusty floor, the stained walls. She could just make out the scratches the chain must have made when the man had obviously fought for his life, but other than that there was nothing.

Claire stood up, walking slowly around the gloomy, even creepy space.

Her slow steps brought her to the wall in front of the window. It had been boarded up, cheap chipboard laying flush with the wall. Again, she used her flashlight, shining its thin beam onto the light brown square, tracing its edges, playing the light back and forth.

Wilson came and stood beside her.

"Anything?" he asked, rubbing his arms with his hands. She felt the same, like the basement had its very own chill that worked its way into your bones as soon as you set foot in it. She wondered if guarding their car was the only reason the police officer had opted to allow them to come down here on their own.

"Don't know…" she said, her eyes squinting, her brow furrowed. There was something…

The beam settled on the top right-hand corner. A gleam of silver reflecting the flashlight.

Stepping closer, she shone the flashlight at the other three corners, the same silver reflection happening each time.

"Look at this," she said, her face inches from the corner of the chipboard. "These are freshly done. This board is too thin to be for security. There's only one reason this has been put up."

She turned to Wilson who was leaning forward studying the screws spotlighted in the circular pool of light.

"Privacy," he said.

"Exactly. Which also means this was premeditated. The killer prepared this basement knowing what he was going to do."

They looked at each other, both thinking what advantage this gave them over the man who had fixed the boards to the window frames.

Claire got there first. "Which means… if we could find another window recently boarded up, we might be able to preempt the killer's next move," she said, her mind going back to her thoughts at the airport, about how detective work was often just a race to discovering the killer's motivation and process.

"Denver's a big place…" Wilson said, "but you're right. It's *something*. Come on let's get out of here."

The two walked back to the corridor, flicking the light off on their way. Even the dank foyer was a welcome relief after the grimness of the basement.

The officer was leaning against the wall, and Claire was sure his eyes had been closed when she first noticed him.

He pushed himself off the wall and quickly looked out at their car.

"All safe and sound out there. See everything you wanted?" he asked, tugging his pants up.

"Yes, for the time being," Claire said, stepping up in front of him. "The board on the window, it's very recently done. Almost certainly by the perp in an attempt to conceal his actions."

She watched as he tried to conceal the surprise on his features. He shuffled his feet.

"If this is part of the killer's MO, then I want you to send out a warning to all officers in Denver and the surrounding area to check for freshly boarded up windows. Basement windows especially."

The officer gave his routine pause before replying. "Denver is a big place, agent. There are a hell of a lot of buildings, and plenty are in a state of disrepair. Not sure my captain is gonna be over the moon having his men walking around looking at renovation works." He gave his pants a yank. "'Specially when there's plenty of other crime in this city."

"Officer," Claire said, pulling herself up to her full height, a height that she was happy to find was an inch taller than the policeman, "by trying to find those recently boarded up windows, not only are we likely to find the individual who did that," she pointed down the stairs into the dark basement, "but also prevent him doing it again. Which, unless things are very different in this city, is *precisely* what the captain should be prioritizing. If you feel differently, please let me know and I can speak to the captain about it myself."

She turned on her heel and strode out, not wanting to hear the man's response. She could imagine what he would be calling her back at the station.

Outside, both found themselves breathing the cool thin air. The car was where they had left it, though being observed by three teenagers at the end of the block.

"Progress," Claire said as she settled into the passenger seat and buckled up. "The key to this case has to lay with those two bodies at the coroners."

"I hope you're right, partner. Either way, we'll know in half an hour."

CHAPTER FOUR

The sheer number of bodies on gurneys that filled every available space was an arresting sight. The Chief's words of it being a war zone rang again in Claire's ears as her eyes got used to the gloom and took in the grim scene.

Her job meant that she had been in dozens of coroners' offices, had seen perhaps hundreds of dead bodies, in various states of injury and dismemberment. But it was the way that these were crammed into the dank, miserable space that made Claire's stomach stiffen. It brought back memories of the old horror films she had watched as a young teenager. Invariably set in some Gothic mansion, or Victorian hospital, the horror on the small television in her room took over from the one being played out in her own house that she shared with her increasingly distant, increasingly drunk, and increasingly menacing father.

Two men in white coats were at the far side of the room. They had buzzed Claire and Wilson in, but had not acknowledged their presence since the two agents had walked through the door. Claire was always impressed by the way coroners went about their grisly work. Efficient, emotionless, methodical. But that was not the impression that exuded from the two in this lab. Anything but. Disorder, stress, and exhaustion were the overriding emotions that came through their erratic, hurried movements, barked instructions, clumsy actions.

As Claire and Wilson approached the two men, she noticed a strange gleam in their eyes that set her on edge. The taller of the two, a man with graying hair and a thick mustache, looked up from the body he was examining and fixed her with a cold stare.

"Can we help you?" he asked, his voice laced with a hint of hostility.

"We're with the FBI," Wilson said, flashing his badge. "We're here to investigate the murders of the two men found chained to radiators. Daniel Walsh and a John Doe."

The shorter man, who had been hunched over a microscope, straightened up at the mention of the murders. He was younger than his colleague, with a bald head and a goatee that failed to disguise his weak chin. He exchanged a quick glance with his colleague then returned to the instrument in front of him.

A silence fell over the room again, only broken by the quiet words the taller of the men spoke into his recording device as he extracted what looked like a nine caliber round from the chest of the man laid out in front of him. Claire watched as the coroner carefully placed the bullet into a small evidence bag, expecting to get his attention when it had been sealed and placed in the appropriate tray.

Instead, he busied himself with another entry wound, this time in the abdomen.

"Look," Claire said, stepping around a gurney, the cadaver covered with only a black foot visible, and towards the coroner. "I appreciate you are busy, but we need to speak to you about those two victims. Then we'll get out of your hair."

The man visibly tensed.

"Look, agent," he said, almost spitting the words out, the word 'agent' spoken as if it was something unpleasant in his mouth he wanted rid of, "it may have escaped your notice but we are having something of a… situation here right now. You can't just fly in from whatever jurisdiction you've come from and expect us to drop everything. You'll have to wait your turn like everyone else."

He went back to the body in front of him, cursing loudly and gruffly when the tweezers slipped from his fingers.

"Yes, I wasn't suggesting we jump the queue. Can you tell me if you have processed our John Doe?" Claire asked. She hated using such a clinical term but, at this moment, it wasn't time for niceties or even subtlety.

The instrument slipped from the medic's fingers again and he ejected another curse, kicking the metal stanchion of the gurney for good measure. He picked the thin metal instrument up from the floor, hurled it into the tray in front of him, and gave Claire a stare that would have frozen champagne.

Claire stared back, trying to keep frustration and aggression away from her eyes, but not wanting to show weakness.

Yes, this man was busy, but their job was no less important. You could argue that gang violence was less time sensitive. It was not in the coroner's office that the problem was going to be sorted out. It was the problems in the schools and the government offices that had led to these unfortunate people ending up in this miserable place. The two bodies they were interested in, however, could very well prevent another joining them in the next day or two.

But it was pointless going down that route. Diplomacy was another skill she'd had to learn. Knowing when to go on the front foot, and when to bite your lip. This was a time for the latter.

The man strode over to a desk in the corner of the room, pulling off his nitrile gloves, and chucking them into the waste box on the floor.

He picked up a clipboard just visible under a sheaf of notes and angrily flipped over the top sheet, his finger tracing the names down.

"B1359. No. Probably isn't gonna be anytime soon either, especially if people keep coming and interrupting." He slammed the clipboard back on the desk and strode back to the gurney, pulling a new set of gloves from a box on the side.

Wilson came and stood next to Claire. They looked at one another, both knowing it was pointless pushing further at this moment.

Claire took a deep breath, the acrid tang of formaldehyde and blood catching at her throat that had only just recovered from being scorched at the Moynahan house. Her eyes roved around the room. The wall on the far side was taken up by a large refrigerator unit, like a huge metal chest of drawers that went from the floor to the ceiling.

She went over to it, aware of the taller coroner steadfastly ignoring her, while the eyes of his younger companion flicked up from the microscope.

Above each metal handle was a small whiteboard with the details of the body that lay within the recess. She scoured the morbid bank of drawers, each containing a body, a life no longer being lived. A story. She was all too aware many would not have anyone to care what their story was.

She was looking for the reference number the coroner had given her, but her eyes were halted when, on the drawer of the bottom row to her right, the name Daniel Walsh leaped out at her. The first victim, the one that had been 'processed.'

She bent down and pulled the handle. After a slight resistance, it slid out, revealing the body she had seen pictures of from the numerous photographs. Some were taken where he had been found, chained to the radiator in a dark and dank basement, very similar to the one they had been in just a an hour before. Others were taken in this very room.

She could feel the eyes of at least one of the coroners on her but ignored it. They had their jobs to do; she had hers.

Daniel Walsh had not improved since those last photographs had been taken. His skin had become more mottled and blotchier, the flesh looking more like something that had been made in a factory than had been grown and nurtured in a mother's womb.

Despite the horrors that lay just below it - the large Y shaped incision that had been done by the coroner before being crudely stitched up – the face looked tranquil. The eyes were shut and the expression was almost one of repose.

Claire's eyes took in the details, not sure what she was looking for. The hairline, receding, a small scar just above the temple. The slightly bent nose. The five o'clock shadow on the cheeks and chin, that she knew would have grown since the man had drawn his last breath.

The lips, strangely pouting, reminded her of some of the young women she saw on advertised television shows. Shows she would rather spend her evenings alone in this room than watch. Her eyes went down to the man's neck, when they suddenly froze and returned to the mouth.

The lips were definitely swollen. Before she knew what she was doing she reached out to touch them, to see if there was anything behind them, anything to cause the puffiness.

As soon as her fingertip touched the cold, unyielding pink flesh, she was hit with a sudden torrent of images, one on top of the next, rushing at her from a long black tunnel.

A man screaming, his mouth distended, his features distorted with the effort. There was no sound, but she could sense the ferocity of the noise ejected, forcing her to recoil.

She also could sense that it was not a scream of fear. It was one of rage. Pure rage. She felt like her body had been dropped into a vat of ice. The rage was palpable, chilling her to the bone, into her bones, into her very being.

Then the face disappeared, as abruptly as it had appeared, replaced by the inside of a dark, dingy basement. Her mind focused on a boarded up window, the gleam of new screws the only brightness, reflecting the light from a source behind her.

Then she was back in the coroner's office. She had sagged under the weight of the vision, both hands gripping the cold steel of the gurney Daniel Walsh was laid upon. The dead man's face now only inches from her own.

As she sucked in gulps of air, she could taste the fluid that his body had been washed with.

A hand on her shoulder, strong but gentle, steadied her from falling any further or from jerking up.

She recognized Wilson's touch, her mind still too confused and startled to understand any significance in *that* realization.

"Claire…? You OK?" His voice was low, but urgent.

She swallowed, felt her heart pounding in her chest. Then she tensed her arms and pushed herself up, away from the sightless face below her. There would be a time shortly to revisit what had happened, but here and now was not that time.

Her mind, settling like her heart, raced back to a few seconds – minutes? – ago. Her eyes went back to the face of the dead man below her. To the lips which seemed to be in the process of reaching out to kiss her. She swallowed her revulsion, and pointed to them with an index finger she was relieved to see did not shake.

"Look at the mouth, the lips," she said.

Wilson bent down closer, his brow furrowed as he followed her instruction.

Claire knew that Wilson had seen almost as many dead bodies as she had. She was willing to bet he had never seen the mouth take on that shape, especially the mouth of a middle-aged male cadaver.

Another presence joined them.

Claire turned to see that the older, taller coroner had given in to curiosity and made his way over to the refrigerator bank. She could still feel the tense energy in his body.

She pointed to the lips.

"I can't remember reading anything in the report about the mouth or lips. Is this something that has happened since?" she said, giving him an out more to ease their own interaction than to save his embarrassment.

The coroner pushed himself in between the two agents, resentment and exhaustion on his face, but unable to resist the chance of putting right anything that questioned the quality of his work.

He paused when he saw the man's mouth, his own lips already open to deliver what was no doubt a comment on people sticking to their own areas of expertise.

He leaned closer, a puzzled look on his face now, and gently parted the lips. He took a pair of tweezers from his breast pocket, and slowly, forcibly opened the man's mouth, the jaw and flesh resisting this foreign intrusion.

The coroner's head was almost touching that of Daniel Walsh, making it look like he was about to give him mouth to mouth.

He was muttering something under his breath, but Claire and Wilson stood back, giving him his space.

The coroner inserted the long thin metal tweezers into the mouth. The teeth were open slightly, but he had to force them open, making

Claire think that she had suddenly found herself in the nightmares of someone with a phobia of dentists.

Two minutes of searching and probing revealed nothing, and Claire could not help but feel that she was about to receive a stern rebuttal to once again keep to her area of expertise, if not her own geographical territory, regardless of the word 'federal' in her job title.

Then the metal probing moved to the area between the teeth and the lips. The hand stopped; the attitude of the coroner's body froze.

All three watched as the steady hand withdrew from the mouth. Clasped in between its delicate jaws was something Claire hadn't seen since junior high science class.

He dropped them into the open palm of his other hand.

Metal shavings, what Claire presumed were iron filings.

"How did they get there?" Wilson asked.

The coroner, his frustrations of earlier seemingly forgotten, returned the tweezers to the mouth.

Two minutes later the pile of shavings had tripled in size.

The coroner asked his assistant, who had torn himself away from the microscope, to bag them. Then he stepped to the middle of the bank of drawers, his eyes and fingers searching for the name he was looking for.

The drawer containing the John Doe, the second man found chained to the radiator, was at head height.

As soon as the body was hauled out, all four peered over, examining the man's lips.

Claire couldn't decide if the mouth of this man showed the same swelling she had noticed on Daniel Walsh. It certainly wasn't as pronounced; the reaction the shavings had produced in the gums and lips of the first victim not having had as much time with the second. Plus the upper lip was masked by a large moustache.

The coroner inserted the tweezers and almost immediately came back out with a clump of the same filings.

CHAPTER FIVE

His thick fingered hands gripped the steering wheel so hard it turned his knuckles white and made his steering jerky. His eyes were fixed on the minivan in front, his eyes like lasers, burning through the rear window into the happy scene inside.

The scene inflamed his rage even more. His hands gripped tighter. His knee twitched. Spittle shot from his mouth along with the oaths and flecked the inside of the windshield. His head leaned closer and closer.

He could feel the anger inside him ready to explode. A volcano of rage, a ball of magma in the pit of his stomach. It took all his effort not to slam his foot down on the gas and ram the back of minivan. That would show them.

His foot even twitched, ready to obey the dark thoughts swirling around his brain.

But he managed to stop himself. Somewhere deep down inside him, a voice made itself heard over the music that blasted through the car's speakers. A voice of reason. Or as near to reason that he could ever produce.

It wasn't a voice that was very vocal. And even when it did give vent to its feelings, its advice was rarely heeded. But this time its message got through.

This was not part of the plan. If he wasn't careful, if he gave vent to his rage too early, everything would be ruined.

The red stoplight turned to green, and he watched, his hands gripping ever tighter, his eyes staring ever harder, as the minivan moved off.

He watched the asphalt stretch out between him and the minivan. Stretch like a piece of elastic, the tension increasing every second. Ready to snap.

A blast of a horn from the SUV behind snapped his eyes to the rear-view mirror. He turned around in his seat and unleashed a volley of fury at the offending driver. Again it took remarkable restraint not to climb out of the vehicle and show the numbskull exactly what he thought about his horn.

But that too would ruin his plan. And the plan was the most important thing. The *only* important thing.

The SUV overtook his still stationary vehicle, and he watched it go, snarling at the driver who was intent on ignoring him now, realizing he had almost messed with the wrong man.

He eased away from the junction, his eyes still focused on the minivan ahead, though there were three other vehicles in between them.

This was better. Safer.

The buildings slid by the freeway. Hoity-toity banks that required more money to open an account than he would ever have in his lifetime. Restaurants whose books would all be full if he tried to darken their doors.

He knew the junker he was driving stuck out in this part of the city. It got looks, the same way a classic Chevy Corvette would in his neighborhood.

Every stare, every smirk, every insult perceived or actual just added to his sense of alienation. But that was what fed his anger. His bitterness. His hatred and rage. That was what drove him. What made him strong.

The minivan ahead made a left turn.

He rolled his shoulders, easing the tension that was building up out of his torso, down his arms. He flexed his fingers on the wheel.

He made the left turn, glowering at a cyclist who he forced to take evasive action onto the sidewalk to avoid his rust speckled motor.

The music, heavy, industrial sounds of guitar strings being thrashed, drumskins being beaten, and vocal cords being shredded, filled the interior of the vehicle. His body twitched and his head nodded in time with the beat.

Outside, the corporate buildings gradually gave way to residential ones. Large properties with names, not just numbers. Sweeping driveways. Gates. Front lawns the size of small parks.

There was a clear road between the minivan and him now, but he kept his distance. His heavy breathing caused his chest to heave as he peered at the vehicle sixty yards in front.

In his mind, he imagined the happy, easy conversation going on in the minivan. Mother and son laughing about some family joke. Perhaps the boy was saying some stupid thing that had happened at his school and his mom was pretending to be impressed or amused.

He slammed the heel of his hand into the door, the cracked plastic cracking a little bit more.

The gaps between the houses on either side of the tree lined road grew larger. The front lawns greener. More landscaped.

Then the buildings gave way to a park and the minivan slowed before making another left turn into a parking lot.

He killed the stereo, the almost silence hitting him with a jolt, then slowed, turned in himself, and found a space away from where the minivan had pulled in.

He killed the ignition, then gripped the wheel again, flexing his fingers, watching in his dirty mirrors what was going on.

There were a group of boys excitedly talking and gathered around three young men, while a few other parents looked on. The two occupants from the minivan climbed out, the woman carrying a catcher's mitt, the boy a baseball bat. They joined the throng, the boy dancing around excitedly, swinging the bat.

His eyes left them briefly, going to a baseball field a hundred yards further away, a white banner with Little League stretched across the chain-link fence.

Then he sought out the woman again, the one who had driven the minivan.

Seeing her chatting easily, shooting the breeze without a care in the world made his rage almost spill over, but then the thought of how he was going to change all of that almost made him smile. He thought about the boy finding out what had happened and his lips stretched into what was as near to a smile as he could produce.

He took a deep breath and rolled his shoulders again. Then his right hand reached over to the seat beside him. He moved the tattered magazine revealing what was underneath.

He flexed his fingers again as his eyes played over the set of handcuffs.

CHAPTER SIX

Claire slammed the phone down, unable to hide her frustration.

They had left the coroner's an hour ago, the two harassed men finally getting their wish to be left in peace with the growing backlog of bodies. Claire had refused to budge before she had extracted as near to a guarantee as she knew she would get that the metal shavings would be sent to the lab for analysis and the second victim, the John Doe, would be processed.

Claire and Wilson got themselves an office at the Denver precinct, settled in, and started going through the case notes – such as they were – before she could wait no longer and rang the coroner's office.

The news had not been good. The shavings *had* been sent for analysis, and they *had* fast-tracked them as much as they were able. What they had not done was get around to processing the second victim. Nothing as explicit was said, but Claire very strongly suspected there was pressure coming from above, from the very top of Denver's political glitterati, to prioritize the gang violence. It was making national news.

When anyone turned on their televisions across America, perhaps even all across the world, the first thing they saw was another shooting in Denver. The DA and the mayor would do anything in their power, and several things not in it, to make sure they turned that negative publicity into something they could hang a hat on as to righting wrongs, helping their community.

Claire was not naïve enough to misunderstand just how the world worked, but it did not make it any less frustrating.

"Nothing doing?" Wilson asked, his tone suggesting he knew precisely how little was being done.

"I feel that half the time we are battling against the criminals with one arm, and the authorities with the other," she said massaging her temples with her thumb and finger.

"Don't forget the leg tied behind our back as well, Claire."

She sighed. She tried not to let her frustrations blow over, and especially not to someone who she still considered to be a junior member of staff.

"Well, it just means we need to double down on what we do. We normally cover several people's work; another couple added on top shouldn't make much difference."

The room they had been given was a self-contained office. Twenty feet by twenty, with a water dispenser in the corner and a square table in the middle, complete with four chairs, comprised the only furniture. But it was private and meant they could work undisturbed.

A window opened out across the football stadium, and then across the colored plains to the mountains in the distance. It was spring, and the sky was a brilliant blue, real heat coming from the burning sun. But Claire knew from bitter experience that the weather in Denver could catch you out.

On a trip to the city some years before, she had gone to bed one night sunburned to wake up the next morning to several inches of snow.

The two agents sat across the table from each other, their laptops on the laminated surface. Photographs, printed files, and sheets filled with handwritten notes lay scattered across the rest of the surface. There was just enough space for their coffee mugs.

With still no ID for the second victim, and his body still lying untouched at the coroner's, the only place to try to uncover anything that might point to a possible perp or motive was with the first one. Daniel Walsh.

They had read through what they had been given, but both knew that no matter who you were, no matter how you tried to remain hidden from society's prying eyes, it was near impossible in the digital information age.

They had split up their point of attack, Claire going at it from the landlord side of Walsh's life, Wilson covering everything else.

Claire had just pulled up the details on the tenement block Walsh rented out when her cell rang.

She snatched it up.

"Agent King,"

"Agent, it's Deputy Chief Flannagan."

Claire pictured the ruddy face of the man she had briefly spoken to earlier. He hadn't seemed overly friendly at the request she had put in, but she got the impression he would be efficient, and she'd take efficiency over friendship any day of the week. She hoped her instincts would be born out over the next couple of minutes.

"Yes deputy, any news?"

"Of sorts, agent," he said, the static of his radio squawking in the background. "Every officer on patrol has been issued with instructions to check for basement buildings with what looks to be newly boarded-over windows."

There was a pause, and Claire could sense he was trying to think of a way to continue.

"But I don't have to tell you that, at the moment, this is not my, my chief's, or my officers' priority. When my men are on the ground, they have a hell of a lot more to worry about than looking for signs of renovation..."

"That said," he said, raising his voice, correctly anticipating an interruption from Claire, "that said, agent, I fully realize the gravity of your situation, and am confident my men will carry it out to the best of their abilities."

Claire sighed. She had expected little else, and to be fair to Flannagan, he had done all she had asked of him.

"Thank you," she said, keeping her voice polite, "though I would add that this isn't 'our situation,' deputy. Someone has killed two residents of *your* city. Whoever it is, they are not likely to stop until they are caught. You don't need me to tell you that right now, this city is under the spotlight of every media outlet in the country. It won't go unnoticed if you have a serial killer on the loose."

"I am fully aware of that, agent," the deputy's voice was curt.

"Thank you deputy, I know you couldn't have done anything else. Please let me know as soon as any of your men report anything that may be of interest. Anything."

Claire put her cell back on the table, and looked over her laptop to Wilson who was eyeing her from the other side of the table, his eyebrows raised.

"Everyone has been instructed to be on the lookout for newly boarded-up windows but..."

Wilson nodded. "It's all we can do at this stage Claire. You know that. And you never know, something might come up."

She gave her head a little shake, as if to mentally shuck off one more frustrating conversation and open her mind to hone in on the immediate problem.

Her eyes focused once again on the image on her laptop screen.

The block was strikingly similar to the one they had visited earlier that day *and* the one where Daniel Walsh had been found dead. That had to mean something. It couldn't be a coincidence, could it? Or was it merely because it was a scenario taking place in a part of the city where those types of blocks were prevalent?

It could have been a building from any large US town or city. Functional rather than aesthetic. A box for humans to live in, designed and built to house as many of them as cheaply as possible. Claire understood that there was nothing wrong with that principle at all; it was the way such buildings were subsequently managed which was where the problems almost always started.

And from what she could gather, that was exactly what had happened in the case of the one on her screen. Via a complicated arrangement, Daniel Walsh was the landlord of all thirty-six apartments in the block. He didn't own the building, but leased it himself from the local authority. Walsh was not only the man responsible for setting the rent for each tenant and ensuring that rent was collected, but also the person responsible for maintaining the block and the apartments to a state where they were fit to live in.

Even from Claire's preliminary research, all three of those factors were a cause of friction between Walsh and the tenants. Often when they found a murder victim, trying to ascertain a motive, a reason *why* anybody would want to kill them, was hard.

That was certainly not the case with Daniel Walsh. Claire imagined every one of the tenants who had been forced to live in squalid conditions had to pay an increasingly high rent to do so, and then endure what could only be described as aggressive tactics when that rent fell behind, would have imagined killing Mr. Walsh at some stage.

Of course, imagining it, even hoping for it, and actually doing it were completely different things.

Someone had made that step, however.

She brought up the file of Daniel Walsh's email correspondence. He'd set up a business which was basically himself, to manage his landlord duties. The email account for that business looked like it would bear fruit. So much fruit, it was difficult to know where to start harvesting.

Walsh must have spent a lot of his time arguing, cajoling, and threatening his tenants. The number of emails both ways showed an impressive commitment to chasing down every minor annoyance. Claire couldn't help but think if he had shown that much commitment, and committed that much energy to maintaining the apartments, half of the problems documented in the emails wouldn't have arisen.

She scrolled down the dozens, probably hundreds of emails, and made a decision.

"How are you getting on?" she asked.

Wilson blew his cheeks out, leaned back in his chair, and cracked his knuckles.

"I dunno. There's either nothing on this guy, he did absolutely nothing, or I'm just not finding it," he said.

"Don't worry about that. I've got more than enough for both of us to trawl through. I'm sending you over a file. It's Walsh's correspondence with his tenants. Let's just say he wouldn't have been winning any landlord of the year awards. There's a lot of anger on both sides. Whether there's evidence someone was capable of crossing the line…"

"There's only one way to see. At least it's something to work on. I've…" he lifted his palms up to the ceiling, "… got nothing on my end."

Claire split the file in two and emailed it to Wilson.

"Woah…" Wilson said, two minutes later, his eyes scanning the emails, "I see what you mean."

A silence settled over the room, only broken by the tapping of keys and the occasional cracking of Wilson's knuckles.

Claire let her eyes scan the correspondence, reading them without reading them, a technique she had developed over the years. Her mind would cry out and keep her finger over the cursor if it spied anything worth further investigation.

At this stage she was just building a file of potential red flags.

The file grew and grew.

An hour later she had exhausted her stack of emails and went back through the ones she had sifted out.

One name jumped out immediately.

Jonny Cairns.

The exchanges between landlord and tenant were particularly hostile. It seemed Cairns had carried work out on his apartment, work that he had repeatedly asked Walsh to do. After taking matters into his own hands, he had then refused to pay his rent up to the amount he had taken off for the work he had done.

It escalated over several months and dozens of emails. Interesting though all that was, it was an email sent two months ago that particularly piqued Claire's interest.

In response to Walsh sending an eviction notice, Cairns had sent a meme of a man in a desert digging his own grave.

"Wilson, take a look at this," Claire said, turning her laptop around to face her partner.

"Wow. That's explicit enough! What's his name? Let's do some digging on this character."

They spent the next fifteen minutes going through everything they could find on Jonny Cairns.

He seemed to have drifted around the greater Denver and Colorado area for several years before finally settling at the block run by Walsh, eighteen months ago.

The two seemed to have been at each other's throats almost from day one. The exchanges had escalated, resulting in the barely concealed death threat and Cairns moving out, still with debts owed, to a new house.

The rest of Cairns's history didn't make for particularly enlightening or uplifting reading, but on a trade website Claire suddenly spotted something that rang alarms bells. Loud alarm bells.

She quickly consulted her own notes then slapped the table triumphantly.

"Gotcha!"

"What have you found?" Wilson said, leaping up from his chair and jogging around to Claire's side of the table.

She pointed to Cairns's resume on the trade site. One of the ways – at least the legitimate ways – Cairns had earned a living was being a handyman. It was, she guessed, why he had become especially frustrated about the circumstances in his own apartment.

On the list of the projects he was responsible for, one name stood out.

Claire pointed to it on the screen. "Ring any bells?"

It was the tenement building where Daniel Walsh had been found. Dead, chained to a radiator.

CHAPTER SEVEN

Claire could feel the tension in the city. It grew as they drove from their hotel to Jonny Cairns's place. As the graffiti and boarded-up store fronts increased, so did the feeling that they were sitting on a dam that was about to break. Groups of men hung about on street corners, waiting for it to break, or wondering what the hell they could do to *make* it break.

She could see Wilson beside her, eyeing the men nervously, especially when they were at red lights. Even if they weren't taken for feds – which it seemed so obvious to Claire that they were – they would still be seen as the enemy. The people with money. With power. Those who had everything, and in turn would do everything to ensure that those without would never get their hands on what they had.

Cairns lived on a street a mile or so from the block where Daniel Walsh had been found. A little over three miles from the one they had visited earlier. They pulled up to the bottom of the hill his house sat on, halfway up.

If anything, this was more run-down than where they had been before. The only two businesses that were not closed down or shuttered up were a clinic dispensing methadone and a liquor store. A long snake of shuffling, twitching men – impossible to age – led to the first of those, a gaggle of men crouched or stood menacingly around the second.

But those two establishments were not the only places of trade and commerce.

In the three minutes it took them to locate the street, wait for the lights to change, and pull up, they witnessed a handful of transactions taking place between a dealer on the corner of the block. A boy on a bicycle, probably no older than eight and no doubt the man's runner, took something from him, circled around their idling sedan, flipped them the bird, and leisurely made his way off in the direction they had come.

"Welcome to paradise," Wilson said, checking the back seat to ensure there was nothing there.

They got out of the car. The dealer who stood on the other side of the intersection showed no interest. A car, driving slowly down the hill, distorted, loud rap music blaring through its open windows, pulled up at the junction next to them. All four pairs of eyes bore into them. The driver, a heavily tattooed man in a vest with a thick gold chain around his neck gave Claire a slow, knowing nod, a smirk playing at his lips.

A man in the backseat mimed cocking a gun with his hand at them.

Claire watched the car drive away slowly, then her eyes went to the sidewalk opposite. Between a charred and closed laundromat and another building so heavily graffitied it was impossible to know what its use had once been, was a small alley. Two men, one tall and musclebound, the other small and wiry, slipped out of it and stood, legs apart watching these two newcomers to the neighborhood.

Claire caught their eyes, aware that neither flinched, both daring her to make the first move.

She looked away, the way she had learned to do with a friend's cat to show you weren't aggressive. She would never normally allow anyone to get the upper hand in this situation, but realized that this was not the time or place to start anything.

Pick your battles Tyler had always said, and this was not her battle. She looked back at the men who were still staring; the smaller of the two was rolling his shoulders, like a boxer in the corner, waiting for the referee to call him to the center of the ring.

"Afternoon gentlemen," Wilson said, treating them to a toothy grin. Any pretense as to what their job was disappeared into the electrified atmosphere.

The tall man, in his early twenties, spat on the ground in front of him, his eyes on Wilson's.

Claire turned up the hill, making her way with easy, steady steps, glad of the comforting presence of her revolver strapped to her shoulder. She heard Wilson behind her humming a tuneless melody.

Cairns's house was sixty yards up on the left. It wasn't a particularly steep slope, but halfway up, both agents were feeling it.

"This altitude..." Wilson said, puffing like he had just finished a run, "rears up and punches you in the gut, don't it?"

Claire nodded, choosing not to waste any precious oxygen on words.

A dog that looked like it was a mix of every breed in the city ran out from a piece of scrubby vegetation on their right. It stood in the middle of the asphalt looking at them, his legs stiff and braced. Then with a gruff bark it loped off down the hill.

Wilson stopped suddenly, pulling at her arm so she did likewise. She looked up at her partner, questioning him.

He took a breath, clearly deciding how to broach something he wasn't one hundred percent comfortable with broaching.

"Look, Claire, earlier in the coroner's…"

She sighed, surprised at the timing, "Are we really going to do this now?"

"I didn't want to say anything; I was waiting for you to bring it up, but you haven't so… I don't want to be in the dark about anything. You owe me that. If you saw something that has a bearing on what we are gonna be walking into up there," he pointed in the direction of Cairns's house, "then I should know. That's all."

The pair locked eyes for several seconds. Then Claire nodded. He was right. She should have said something sooner; it was just the uncertainty that she still felt around the whole thing.

"Yes. Yes, you're right. Sorry Wilson, I *should* have said something, but don't think it was a deliberate decision. To be honest, there's not a great deal to tell."

She closed her eyes, trying to bring back into focus the images she had seen, the emotions she had felt. It was an uncomfortable journey back into the recesses of her mind.

"There was a man, the man responsible, I'm sure. He was yelling. Screaming. At me, or whoever… whoever I was. He was so angry. So angry. We were in a basement, like the one we saw… I don't know if it was the same one… it was all too quick, too indistinct. But it did have boarded-up windows. I even saw the new screws."

"You saw the man! Can you remember his face?" Wilson said excitedly.

"No… it was all… all too quick." She sighed, struggling to put into words exactly what she had gone through. "I didn't really see his face. Or I did, but it was so angry; he was yelling, that was what I saw. But I couldn't hear him… look I know I'm making no sense, but that is the best I can explain it."

"Would you recognize him? Is it Cairns?"

She shook her head in exasperation. "I don't think I would, no. I don't know."

Wilson thought for a couple of seconds. "You say you saw the boarded-up window. The new screws. Can you be sure you weren't just remembering what we had seen earlier?"

Claire's hand went to her head, massaging the skin either side of her eyes. "I don't think so. It was… I don't know. I think it was different. The angle, the height on the wall. My impression was that it was somewhere else. Somewhere different. But… I couldn't swear that's the case."

Wilson nodded.

She looked back down the hill from where they had come. The two men were still watching them. "Come on," she said and continued up the road.

Cairns's house was a grimy one-story dwelling set back twenty yards from the sidewalk. The front yard had a sofa, one of its cushions missing, the other sporting a large round burn. The drapes on both windows were drawn.

The two agents exchanged a look before approaching the front door. Claire knocked three times, her knuckles rapping against the wood paneling with a hollow sound.

There was the faint sound of a television somewhere inside, but no movement.

She stepped back a couple of yards and studied the house. The black t-shirt beneath her jacket was stuck to her back with sweat - partly due to the exertion of the walk in the thin atmosphere, partly due to the sun that was blazing down on her.

A flicker of movement of the drapes on the right-hand window caught her eye, but she couldn't be sure if she had imagined it or not. Like everything else with the building, the door looked like it had been slowly but dutifully neglected for years, though it did seem to be sporting three newish locks. Security she guessed was paramount around here, and at least he would know how to fit them.

Wilson banged twice more, using his fist.

"Mr. Cairns!" he called.

Claire studied the windows but there was no movement. She turned around, thinking that there would be an audience watching from the sidewalk, but it was deserted.

She stepped forward motioning with her head that she was going to take a look out the back, then made her way slowly around the left-hand side of the house.

A rusty mountain bike was propped up against the gray wall, both tires flat, the front wheel buckled. The back garden was a mixture of overgrown grass and dead, burnt patches. A metal chair lay on its side. The back door didn't look like it had been used since the last summer, but her eyes went immediately to the window that looked out from a square block that looked like an addition to the original building.

The window was open. Here the sound of the television inside was louder. It sounded like a talk show, with only the audience's occasional reaction audible.

Carefully she peaked through the window, but it was frosted. The open portion was across the top. She eyed it, judging if she could fit through, and guessed she would. At a push.

She could hear Wilson banging on the front door, calling for Cairns to open up.

As well as the thought of a potential serial killer on just the other side of the dirty window and thin walls, was the moral one.

If she played this by the book, she should return with a warrant.

But if she played this by the book, Jonny Cairns could very well get away. And if he got away there was a very, very good chance that the place he went to would mean there would very shortly be another body on the slab at the coroner's.

She eyed the window.

She knew she could get away with saying she had heard enough evidence that made her believe there was a crime being committed on the premises. She also knew that if she started going too far down that route – like she had known colleagues to – then the line between the supposed good guys and bad ones grew fainter, ever blurrier.

But she also knew that it was her job, the job she was paid to do, to protect the people of America. So she decided to do whatever she needed for exactly that.

Claire stepped back, seeing if there was any other way into the house. The only other window at the back of the house had a blind drawn. She stepped up to the door, gripped the rusty handle and gently applied some pressure, but it didn't give at all. Locked.

Taking the chair, she stood it under the frosted window, balanced on it, her heart fluttering when it seemed one of the legs might buckle; then she gripped the dirty ledge of the open window with one hand. Reaching in with the other, she found the clasp and opened it as far as it would go, before pushing off with her legs.

It was a squeeze, but she managed to wriggle through, the metal of her revolver pushing painfully into her collar bone.

Quietly, as stealthily as she could, she dropped to the filthy floor below. It was the bathroom. A cracked and flecked mirror on the far wall reflected the scene. A bath sat next to a toilet, the seat cracked. A dozen empty beer cans littered the floor as well as a handful of tattered tabloids.

The noise of the television was louder in here.

She pulled out her gun and stepped out of the filthy bathroom.

CHAPTER EIGHT

Claire stepped into the gloomy hallway. A small kitchen was to her left, its surfaces littered with dirty pots, pans, and plates, as well as empty beer cans. The blinds were pulled down, giving the appearance of evening in the house, despite it still being broad daylight outside.

There were shadows everywhere. Each a potential hiding place. If Cairns was the killer, and she had to believe he was, he would have no qualms about killing her in his house.

The television program cut to an ad break, and over the sound of the benefits of a local car dealership, she could hear Wilson banging on the front door, demanding Jonny Cairns open the door so he could speak to him.

She trod slowly and lightly, easing her way along the soiled vinyl floor towards the room in front and to her left. The front door, reverberating with Wilson's knocks lay straight ahead.

Her eyes darted to the left and right, gradually getting used to the gloom, the shadows, the hiding places retreating from her gaze.

If Cairns was hiding, waiting to strike, he was not doing it in the hallway. Was he still in the living room, from where she saw the drape twitch?

She tried to decide between confronting Cairns herself, or opening the door, letting Wilson in.

Then the decision was taken out of her hands.

Jonny Cairns, wearing dark-gray jogging bottoms and a deep red, shapeless sweatshirt appeared in the doorway of the living room. He was focused on the door to his left, his back to the agent just two yards behind him. Then he must have sensed her presence.

He swung around, his face undergoing a series of expressions: shock, anger, disbelief, then back to anger.

"What the… who the… How…?"

Claire raised her gun, pointing it at the man's chest, drawing his startled eyes away from her face to its steel muzzle.

"Jonny Cairns?" she said, reaching for her badge, her gun never leaving the chest of the man in front of her.

In a move that seemed at odds with his appearance, but one that she guessed was born out of living in the middle of two gang territories in an impoverished part of the city, he flung himself back into the room he had just left, his arm slamming the door.

Her mind raced. Wilson was almost within touching distance, but Cairns almost certainly had a gun somewhere in the house, and she would bet it was in the room where he spent most of his time. The room he had just entered.

Whether he thought she was there to arrest him for killing those two men or that she was a burglar, he'd be extremely motivated to fill her with lead.

A split second after Cairns had made the same move, Claire followed, kicking the door open, then rolling forward and down, her two arms pointing out in front, her finger ready to discharge her weapon.

Cairns was bent over a wooden cabinet, his hands rifling in a drawer.

Claire was on her knees, no more than a yard from the hunched-over figure.

A cheer from the television set mounted on the wall blocked out the sound of her thudding heart.

Cairns swung around, a black large caliber revolver clasped in his hands. Claire launched herself forward and upward, connecting with the thighs and midriff of Cairns, sending him backwards onto and over the cabinet, pinning him to the wall.

His gun went off, deafening Claire. For a split second her body tensed, unsure of where the bullet had gone - if it had thudded into the floor or into her own shoulder.

Her senses came back with a clean bill of health, and she shoved her own gun into the underside of Cairn's chin.

"DROP THE WEAPON!" she screamed into the man's ear, her own still ringing from the gunshot.

She could sense the dilemma going on in the man she had pinned to the wall.

"FBI! DROP YOUR WEAPON!" she shouted again, pushing the muzzle of her gun harder into his chin.

That seemed to do the trick. His body sagged beneath her, then she half-felt, half-heard his gun fall to the floor.

"Good decision," she said, stepping back from Cairns, the gun still held to his throat.

"Claire!" Wilson cried as he rushed into the room, his own gun raised, his eyes quickly surveying the scene in front of him.

"It's ok," she said, her breathing returning to its regular pattern.

"Mr. Cairns is ready to be taken in. One shot discharged. No injuries."

***

The interrogation room at the Denver precinct was almost identical to every other one that Claire had sat in. And she had sat in a lot of them. The only thing that changed was the person opposite her, and occasionally the one next to her.

Jonny Cairns was twitchy. He veered from aggression to fear. The patchy gray growth of stubbly hair that covered his head looked like it had been shaved in the dark, and mirrored his lined, stressed face. It made a scratchy sound when he rubbed his calloused hands over his chin, head, and cheeks which he did repeatedly.

The car had been left untouched when they returned to it, though the two men they had seen earlier had been joined by several more. Claire and Wilson had been watched intently as they led Cairns down the hill and into the car, but no one said anything. She guessed it was not an unusual sight in that neighborhood. Even so, she found herself letting out a relieved sigh when Wilson had maneuvered the car away from the junction and had pointed it in the direction of the precinct.

Apart from the repeated declaration that he hadn't done anything, Cairns had said nothing, and the two agents were happy to wait until they were in the proper setting before he did his talking.

Now, sitting across the table from them, his tongue was no loser.

Claire was happy to wait, to show that they had all the time in the world. From experience, she knew the pressure of being questioned by two members of the FBI would mount on someone like Cairns. He may not be the model citizen, but he had managed to avoid being arrested since a drunken incident in a bar almost twenty years earlier.

"Daniel Walsh, Mr. Cairns. What does that name mean to you?" Wilson said.

Cairn's nervous eyes swung round to his questioner.

"Money grabbing scum," he spat the words out. "That's what that name means to me."

He looked at the two people in front of him. Their neat black jackets and smart hairstyles accentuated his state of disarray.

"Is he why I'm here?" He emphasized the word 'he,' leaving the agents in no doubt as to his feelings towards the man.

Claire hoped that Wilson would play this slowly, like reeling in a fish. There was no point rushing, messing it up by revealing your hand too quickly. That way only led to losing your advantage, to seeing the fish escape the hook and disappear into the depths. She briefly considered stepping in but decided to give her partner the benefit of the doubt. She had to remind herself that he was more experienced than she often gave him credit for.

Wilson reached into a folder in front of him, flicking through a small pile before extracting three sheets of paper. He slid them across the shiny tabletop. Beside him, Claire privately gave a nod of satisfaction. "Well done Wilson," she thought. She had been right to trust him.

Cairns, his eyes on Wilson's, reached across, and pulled the sheets of paper closer, turning them around so he could read them.

It took him a few seconds to recognize them as the transcripts of email exchanges between him and Walsh.

"Where did you get these? Did he give you these?" His anger was mounting.

Wilson waited a couple of seconds.

"Can you confirm these are emails that you sent and received from Daniel Walsh?"

"Yeah, but I don't know what they have to do with anything?" Cairns shoved the sheets back across the table, his face accusatory.

Wilson picked them up, looking at them as if they were the most interesting thing he had seen for a good while.

"You carry on like this," he read, "and you'll live to regret it. Believe me. You're messing with the wrong man." He turned to another page and held it up for Cairns to see. It was a still of the meme of a man digging a grave in the desert. "Do you know what these are Mr. Cairns?" he asked, then continued, before Cairns could realize it was a rhetorical question. "Let me tell you exactly what they are. They are death threats."

Cairns spat out an indignant noise.

"Death threats. Pah! Just words. It's ok for the big men in the high glass towers to say these things. Worse. To carry out and do them. It's them that you should be going after. They're the ones that are causing all of this," he swung his hands around, gesturing, Claire guessed, to the whole city. "People like me send a couple of emails and…" He shook his head angrily. "Is that really why you broke into my house and dragged me all the way here? I could sue…"

"The reason we brought you down here Mr. Cairns," Claire said, leaning forward in her seat, "is because Daniel Walsh, the man you admit to threatening in those emails, was found dead. He was murdered."

Cairns looked at Claire. She could see his brain trying to digest the information. His forehead creased with the effort. She waited, letting him work it out for himself, while she studied the man in front of her. Was he faking his confusion? Was he so far adrift from reality that he didn't even know or remember killing those men? Or was he actually innocent?

"Murdered?" he said, the aggression gone. Then realization finally dawned on him. "You... you don't think... come on, these were just meaningless emails. I was angry. I wouldn't have killed him over some petty argument."

"Doesn't look to me like it was petty Mr. Cairns," Claire said. She pointed to the emails. " Plus, there is outstanding rent. Pretty easy way to get out of that, wouldn't you say?"

"I wouldn't kill someone for a couple of thousand bucks. Anyway, it isn't outstanding. It's the money Walsh owes me... owed me, for the work I did."

Wilson sat back, his fingers flicking through the folder. He pulled out a color photograph and held it up to Cairns. It was of a building. A tenement block.

"Do you recognize this photograph Mr. Cairns?"

Cairns stared at the picture for a second, visibly shocked at the way events were turning.

He nodded. "Yeah, I do work there from time to time. I'm a janitor at the block."

Wilson returned the photograph to the folder.

"So you have access to the building. You have a set of keys? For the basement, for example?"

Cairns nodded. "Yeah, why? What has this got to do with me? With Walsh? He doesn't own this place."

"That was the building where Daniel Walsh was murdered. In the basement. The basement that you have the keys to."

Cairns put his head in his hands, the calloused skin catching on the coarse stubble.

"Look this is crazy," he said speaking down into the tabletop. "You have got this all wrong."

"Where were you between 3pm and 8pm on the 13th, Mr. Cairns? Last Tuesday," Claire asked.

It took Cairns a couple of seconds to process the question. She really didn't think it was a stalling tactic, but rather the way his brain worked.

He looked up, his eyes scanning the wall behind her, as if searching for the answer to her question.

"Tuesday… I was working. I'm a janitor at the water works off Dempsey. Shift starts at two, goes through to ten."

Claire narrowed her eyes. "Do you have witnesses that will back that up?"

"Yeah," Cairns was suddenly confident again, seeing the momentum of the interview had shifted in his favor. "I clock in. Plus there's two other guys I work with. Now, can I go?" He made to stand up.

"Sit down Mr. Cairns. We will check your alibi. But first," Wilson said, his fingers going back to the folder and taking out another photograph and laying it down on the table in front of Cairns.

It was the face of the second man found chained to a radiator. The John Doe. The picture, taken on the slab at the coroner's, had been cropped to just show the head. The man's eyes were closed. He could have been sleeping, but the metal gurney visible beneath his head made it clear it was a sleep he would not wake up from.

"Do you recognize this man?" Wilson asked.

"Who is it, some other guy I didn't kill?" Cairns's eyes flicked down, disinterestedly to the photograph for a second before looking back at the agent across from him. "No. Never seen him before in my life."

Claire could feel the frustration building inside her. She looked at Cairns who was rubbing his cheeks, his chin, his scalp. His shoulders were pulled back a little now, he didn't look as defeated as he had earlier. Then she saw that familiar crease of his forehead, and his eyes once more traveled to the picture in front of him. His hand reached out, straightening the photo slightly. Another expression crossed his face, like a cloud crossing the sun.

She leaned forward. "*Do* you recognize him?" she kept her voice even, not wanting to sound too desperate, fully aware that he would be in no mood to help them.

Cairns leaned closer. "TJ?"

"TJ?" Claire said. "A friend of yours?"

Cairns studied the picture for a few more seconds, then shook his head.

"Nah… he ain't no friend but I know who it is. Everyone does 'round my way. TJ. Tommy Jacobson, but everyone knows him as TJ."

Claire made a note on her pad.

"He's dead?" Cairns asked picking up the photograph. He didn't sound surprised, or disappointed. He asked the question the same way he would have confirmed the day was Friday.

Claire couldn't see the point in lying. "Yes." Then another thought came to her mind, and she acted upon it, before she could stop herself.

She reached out her hand in the pretense to retrieve the photograph from Cairns' grasp, but touching his thick fingers with her own thinner ones.

The man recoiled from her touch and tossed the photograph onto the table. But there was nothing else. The cell didn't disappear. There was no face thrust at her from the dark. No sounds crashed around the walls. Just plain old normal sanity.

She took a breath to compose herself.

"What else can you tell us about Mr. Jacobson?" she asked, again not wanting to make Cairns withdraw by putting too much importance on the inquiry. He had no reason to help them.

"Nothing to tell. He's another of these landlords. You know the sort. More interested in screwing their tenants out of as many greenbacks as they can than actually doing what's right by the poor souls forced to live in their buildings."

Claire's body tensed and she could sense Wilson doing exactly the same, next to her.

"Tommy Jacobson was a landlord of a tenement block in the city. The same as Daniel Walsh?" she said.

Cairns shrugged, "Yeah, that's what I just said. It's hardly a state secret. Now, I'm bored of this, take me home."

She ignored him and looked at Wilson, making a mental note to tell the local PD they should be looking into landlords and not just recently boarded windows.

In her mind, a triangle had just closed.

CHAPTER NINE

It was time to kill again.

Above his rust speckled, dented Nissan, the sky had darkened from a bright azure blue to a deep navy one. The first stars were starting to show themselves. A thin sliver of moon hung hesitatingly on the horizon.

But he noticed none of that. He was focused on two things and two things only.

Keeping the magma of rage that sat deep in his belly from erupting was the first. The second was watching the events unfold a hundred or so yards away in the park.

He knew the routine, had observed it, noted it before when he had scoped out the means of getting her on her own.

But routines could change. He knew life had a way of pulling the rug out from under you when you least expected it.

So he watched and waited.

The sound of his heartbeat grew louder in his ears, drowning out the distant laughter of children playing in the park. The deeper cheer of parents. Every passing minute, every joyful sound, made the magma in his belly boil up hotter, threatening to bubble over, until it took a supreme effort to stay where he was. In the driver's seat, twitching and flexing, hands stuffed between his legs, his mind counting up to ten over and over, like some broken soundtrack.

From this distance, it was hard to tell what was going on in the game. Hard to stop his mind filling in the blanks, jumping to conclusions as to why the woman hadn't returned to her vehicle. To sort out the refreshments for the kids. Like she always did.

His frantic mind threw up some other potential problems.

What if she got help this time?

What if she was deep in conversation about… about… whatever these types of people talked about. Perhaps she was so deep in conversation, neither person could bear to break off and they would return to the minivan together.

The magma rose up to his chest, and his hands flew to his solar plexus, physically kneading at his flesh to keep it contained.

“One, two, three...” his mind whirred through the loop, concentrating on each number, pushing the thoughts of what could go wrong down into the dark corners of his mind. Where they would find plenty of company.

Suddenly, movement in the park caught his eye. He leaned forward, squinting to get a better view. It was difficult to see in the fading light, but he could make out the silhouette of a figure walking towards the parking lot. He tensed, his heart beating faster. Was it her? Or just some random person leaving the park?

As the figure drew closer, he could see that it was indeed her. His target. She was alone, and he felt a surge of triumph mixed with excitement. This was it. The ball of magma did a little flip, but it was calm, as if it somehow knew it would have an outlet soon. Very soon.

He watched her closely, noting her easy gait, the trace of a smile still on her lips, as if remembering a conversation from just a minute earlier.

He thought, with triumph, that it was going to be the last smile that ever stretched that little mouth of hers.

He watched her approach the minivan, reveling in the knowledge that these would be the last happy, carefree moments of her life.

Knowing that she was so unaware of what was about to happen, he knew exactly what was going to unfold, and not only that but he was master of her destiny, and this empowered him.

His fingers flexed but this time not with tension or frustration. This time it was with excitement. Power. Strength.

His eyes scanned the park from where the woman had come, but there was no one else. No one had run after her, offering to help. No one had seen that she had dropped something and was chasing back to return it.

A cheer from the baseball diamond rolled out over the parking lot.

He gently opened the door. The cool evening air replacing the stale atmosphere that had been trapped in the vehicle. The chill made him realize there was a sheen of sweat on his forehead and his forearms. His hand reached out and grabbed the little pile from the passenger seat.

He slipped out of the car, his head down, but his eyes on the woman twenty yards away.

She had reached her vehicle and had opened the minivan’s rear doors.

His sneakered feet made no noise on the asphalt surface of the parking lot. He controlled his breathing, timing it with the counting in his head, the numbers on their endless loop now being ticked off slower. He was in control now.

He skirted the side of the parking lot, not wanting to go directly to the woman, but to come at her from a more natural angle. Should she happen to turn around, he could disguise his route, if she even saw him.

She was bent over now, rearranging the contents of the two large coolers.

He calculated that he had another twenty seconds, perhaps half a minute.

He was fifteen yards away.

Ten.

She straightened up, stretching and arching her back, her hands pushing into the small of her back, just above her colorful yoga pants.

He could hear her humming now, some tune he recognized from an ad on television.

In a silent, swift movement, that seemed alien to the shape and build of his body, and his hands and fingers, he unscrewed the bottle he held in one hand, placing the cloth over it with the other. All the time careful that the metal of the handcuffs were gripped next to the bottle so they didn't give his position away with a metallic clank.

He was less than five yards away when she sensed or heard him.

She swung around, the quizzical look on her face freezing when she saw him.

He was on her in a flash.

His hand extended and closed around her face. His weight pushed her back, so she fell into the back of the minivan, the rigid plastic of the coolers sharp and hard in her back.

The sweet, almost citrus smell of the chloroform filled his nostrils, and he clamped down harder on her face, the cloth filling her mouth and nose, blotting out the squeals and cries.

She struggled beneath him, her legs and arms clawing at her attacker, beating at him. The cloth covered her eyes though and a lot of her fading energy was wasted pawing the air.

Still he pushed down, pushing over one of the coolers, spilling the foil wrapped contents and bottles of juice.

Her legs left the ground as she fell back into the van, all his weight on her now.

Still she struggled and kicked.

This was the most dangerous time. If someone came now, there was nothing he could do.

But he could feel her strength lessening. Her legs and arms continued but without the ferocity. The grunts from under the cloth were more subdued, less urgent.

Then she was still. Her body limp. He held the cloth in place for a few more seconds, then allowed himself to look over the roof the of the minivan to the park.

There was no one coming. No one had seen or heard a thing.

In a movement he had seen on a thousand cop shows, and now one he had performed three times himself, he clamped the cuffs on first one wrist then the other.

He stood up straight, his eyes searching the gloomy park in front of him for any signs that anyone was heading his way, but there was nothing.

Heaving the limp body of the woman up, the cloth still over her face, he put her over his shoulder and jogged back to his vehicle, resting the body against the side while he quickly opened the rear door, then shoved her inside.

He checked that there was no sign of movement, just the slightly ragged breathing, then he covered her with a filthy blanket, forcing her foot into the footwell so he could close the door.

Throwing the once more stoppered bottle onto the passenger seat, he walked quickly to the driver's side and jumped in.

A quick look in the mirrors showed he was alone in the parking lot.

The sky was now almost black, the deep, deep blue punctured by dozens and dozens of stars.

In the parking lot below, the car backed out. At the junction it turned right, heading back to his part of town. On the backseat the woman's body shifted slightly as the car accelerated away, in a deep, dreamless, pitch black sleep.

CHAPTER TEN

"Cairns's alibi checks out," Claire said, pocketing her phone and nodding at Wilson who was leaning against the wall next to the coffee machine.

She had been expecting it. The way he had delivered it, plus the fact she didn't credit Cairns with the mental dexterity to come up with such a solid alibi on the spot, meant before she had even made the call to the water works, she knew they would confirm Jonny Cairns had been at work the entire window for Daniel Walsh's murder. He had also been working when Jacobson – if the John Doe *was* Jacobson – met his maker.

The interview with Cairns had not been fruitless though. Far from it.

Not only did they have a probable ID for the second victim, they had a connection. What that connection meant, time would hopefully tell, but it was something for them to get their teeth into.

"Come on," Wilson said leading the way to their office.

The city lights were flicking on outside the window as the day gave way to evening, the mountains on the horizon now an indistinct gray smudge. Claire sat down in the chair and flicked open her laptop.

"First step is to see if Tommy Jacobson *is* our man," she said, Wilson leaning on the back of her chair watching as she brought up the man's profile.

If Tommy Jacobson wasn't the man who had been found dead chained to a radiator in a basement and was now lying in a refrigerator unit in the city coroner's office, then he had a doppelganger running around the city.

Wilson walked slowly back to his own seat on the opposite side of the table.

"So," he said. "Two bodies, both landlords. Specifically, both landlords of rundown tenements in the city. Neither of them particularly loved by their tenants as far as we can tell, but then, if you were gonna choose a profession that had a routinely low popularity rating, I guess landlords are right up there with real estate agents and anyone from the IRS."

Claire looked up to the ceiling, stretching her neck and running her hands through her hair. She still wasn't used to its new, short length, and often found her fingers groping for the missing inches.

"OK, do you want to see what you can dig up on Jacobson? There may be a red flag that crops up that triggers something we know about Walsh," she said.

"You gotcha. What angle are you gonna try?"

Claire tapped her fingers on the table top, thinking. "There's got to be a connection. The most obvious one is someone who was a tenant of both Jacobson *and* Walsh. As good a place to start as any."

Walsh was a landlord for one block. Jacobson on the other hand had two currently under his name, and had also been the landlord of another one, that funnily enough had been located next to the one where he was found before being pulled down almost a decade before.

Getting the lists of tenants for all four blocks proved a more straightforward task than Claire had imagined. She started to think that perhaps things were going their way in this investigation. The disappointment of the coroner's office seemed a thing of the past.

She looked down at the list of several hundred names, confident one of them would show that they had, at some time, been subject to both the dead men's rent increases and poor treatment.

It took her twenty minutes to get a match.

It was Maria Rodriguez, a woman who had been evicted by Walsh thirteen months ago, and had then moved into one of Jacobson's properties. Claire sat up, her heart racing with excitement as she pulled up Maria's file, eager to delve deeper into her possible connection to the murders. The name rang a bell, and she skimmed through the data, trying to see where else in the investigation that name had come up.

But nothing jumped out. Maybe she was mistaken. The main thing was that they had one match and there was still half the list to go. Claire hadn't ruled out the perp being a man; there hadn't been overtly physical violence associated with either killing, but she just sensed it had been a man who had carried them out.

She was more than willing to ditch that sense in the face of evidence, however.

She typed Maria Rodriguez into Google, still sure she had heard the name recently. As soon as it came up on the page she remembered exactly where she *had* heard the name and her heart dropped.

Maria Rodriguez had been one of the first victims of the escalating gun violence in the city. She was the innocent victim of a drive by shooting three weeks earlier, catching a stray bullet on her way back from the late night supermarket where she had gone to buy formula for her eight-month-old baby. Being a young mother, the story had made national headlines, as the country's media began to turn its attention to what was going on in the Mile High City.

The rest of the names produced nothing. Many shared the same surname, but a little background digging proved there was no familial connection with any of them.

She crossed the last name off the list and rubbed her eyes, the earlier optimism starting to fade.

From the silence on the other side of the desk she guessed it was a similar story there too.

"Any joy?" she asked, standing up and going to look out the window.

Wilson tapped the pen against his teeth as he contemplated the words on the screen in front of him.

"Dunno…" he said, rapidly typing in a few more search terms, then leaning closer to the laptop. "Maybe…"

Claire turned around, leaning against the window ledge. She reached for her water bottle.

"What you got?"

"Not sure," he said. "Have a look at this."

He turned his laptop towards Claire.

"First of all, I got zilch on Jacobson. He ain't gonna win any awards from real estate monthly, and he rubbed some of his tenants the wrong way, but there's nothing along the lines of what we had for Walsh."

"But…"

"But, then I started looking a bit deeper, going at the landlord angle as opposed to these two specifically. Something Cairns said, about big men in big towers or something along those lines. I thought it was just a throwaway comment, the usual voice of the oppressed, you know, but… I dunno," he looked at Claire, his hands rubbing his hair. "I wanted to see if there *was* anything happening, especially in Denver, and particularly this part of Denver where these two, and landlords like them, seem to operate."

Claire came and crouched down next to her partner, trying to make sense of what she could read on his screen.

"Go on," she said, nodding for him to continue.

"So, I found this…" Wilson pointed to a small article buried in the local news section of a local newspaper. It was dated two months ago.

"There seems to be some friction in the property sector, particularly among the landlords of tenement blocks, between them and this banking group, DPG." He opened another window on the laptop to reveal a standard corporate website.

"Doing a little bit of digging, they seem to be buying up cheap properties in the area."

"Banking on the area being gentrified, I take it. I can't imagine they will be overjoyed with what's going on with these gang turf wars," Claire said.

"Unless they are thinking what's going on will completely clear the area. Bring the prices down, make landlords want to get out. There's more than one person claiming this whole tension has been manufactured for precisely that reason."

"Do you believe that? Any of it?" Claire asked.

"Probably not. But that isn't important, because if enough people do…" Wilson left the sentence hang in the tense silence of the room, while they both thought over the implications of such actions.

"But that's an aside," he continued after twenty seconds. "It's not the fact that this DPG group is buying up properties, or looking to buy up properties. It's the way they are going about it."

"Such as?" Claire was intrigued. This was a completely different angle. Their first assumption had been a disgruntled tenant, but what if the pressure was coming from above, not below?

"I can't find anything explicit, but there is a lot of chatter about underhanded tactics. Very underhanded. DPG has been applying *a lot* of pressure to those landlords holding out. There is even talk of DPG deliberately disrupting power and water supplies to blocks owned by landlords not wanting to sell."

"None of it proven of course," Claire said.

"Yep, none of it proven of course."

Claire stood up. "It turns our thinking on its head," she said, walking slowly around the table, her mind weighing up this new theory. "So it could be some exec at this DPG applying a little bit too much pressure…"

"It could even have been a mistake, a threat that went too far. He may not even have meant to kill them?" Wilson said, following Claire around the room with his eyes.

"Yeah, but if you make that mistake with the first, would you go back and do the exactly same thing again?"

"OK, maybe not." He turned back to the screen. "Their head office is three blocks from here," he said, and looked at his watch. "Almost seven o'clock. Do you think anyone will still be there?"

"There's only one way to find out," Claire said grabbing her jacket from the back of the chair, fully aware that they were not just about to walk into the offices of a bank; they were about to confront the person or people who were responsible for the deaths of two men, and possibly the ones who had deliberately turned the city into powder keg, before sitting back and lighting the fuse.

CHAPTER ELEVEN

"Have you got an appointment? Mr. Woodward is a busy man."

Claire looked at the large man in front of them, behind the reception desk.

He had the appearance of night security as opposed to the primly efficient woman Claire imagined occupied the spot during normal office hours.

The blocks between their office and the banking corporation's head office were a world away from the ones they had visited earlier that day. Corporate offices, featuring acres of polished glass and artwork and sculptures in their foyers worth as much as the apartments in the blocks that Daniel Walsh and Tommy Jacobson were renting out.

DPG itself was less grand, but there was still enough polished chrome in the large reception area for Claire to catch sight of her new short hair from every conceivable angle.

"No we haven't got an appointment; is he here? What floor is he on?" Claire took her badge back and made to go towards the elevators.

"I'm not sure Mr. Woodward is still here. It is late."

Claire turned back to the man, who was still standing. He was in his late forties, maybe early fifties. His suit looked quite expensive, but like it had been made for someone else. She looked at the name badge pinned to his lapel.

"Barney, you have just told me Mr. Woodward is a busy man, and I have absolutely no doubt he is. Which is why I also have no doubt he will still be working." She treated the security man to a smile, that she hoped looked at least partly genuine. "Exactly like you are still working, and exactly like my partner here and I are still working. And I would hazard a guess, that Mr. Woodward's wage packet at the end of every month is considerably larger than all of ours."

Barney stood still, considering her words.

"We also appreciate," Claire went on, "that having federal agents walking through reception, causing a scene is not something that is good for a corporation's image…"

"Or their share price…" Wilson interjected.

"… so we thought it prudent to come… after hours. Of course, if you think Mr. Woodward would prefer to see us, say tomorrow morning at ten o'clock, we would be very happy to accommodate him…"

"Ok, ok, I will call him."

Claire watched as Barney sat down, picked up the desk phone, then spoke quietly into it. She couldn't hear the conversation, but imagined he was repeating her barely veiled threat about publicity.

"Ok," Barney said after replacing the receiver. "Mr. Woodward is available. The sixteenth floor."

After the elevator doors had closed, Wilson turned to Claire and smiled.

"Well handled, agent."

"You know, I almost felt sorry for old Barney," she said returning the smile.

Wilson raised an eyebrow. "Almost?"

Claire shrugged. "Hey, we're just doing our job. And besides, it worked."

As they arrived on the sixteenth floor, they were greeted by a sleek, modern reception area. Claire couldn't help but notice the floor-to-ceiling windows that offered an incredible view of the city's night skyline.

A young woman with a tight bun and a pencil skirt walked quickly from a door just off the reception area, smoothing her skirt with her hands, making Claire wonder just what form Mr. Woodward's work that evening was taking.

"We are here to see Samuel Woodward," Claire said. "He knows we are here."

"Yes of course," the woman said, her eyes assessing Claire's black jacket and trousers, her conclusion as to their price tag written all over her face.

Claire walked past her. "In here?" she said, indicating the room the woman had just walked out of.

Before she could answer, a man of Claire's height with neat gray hair, wearing a suit she guessed cost the equivalent of a couple months' mortgage payments on her apartment, appeared at the door.

"Mr. Woodward?" she said. "I'm agent Claire King from the Federal Bureau of Investigation. This is agent Mark Wilson."

Woodward didn't bother looking at the badge held up for his inspection. He stood, blocking the way into his office, which Claire could see behind him. It also boasted floor to ceiling windows and a couch larger than the one she had at home.

"We could discuss what we have come to speak to you about out here Mr. Woodward, but I am pretty sure what we are going to say is something you would prefer wasn't within the earshot of your…secretary." Claire stood a foot away from Woodward, eyes level and boring into his. In her line of work she rarely got to question individuals like Samuel Woodward.

Most of the people she dealt with thought they were above the law, and that was almost always why their paths crossed. But with the likes of Woodward, that arrogance and entitlement was different. More ingrained.

He held her stare for a couple of seconds, and Claire knew that for the thousandth time in his life, at that moment he was wishing with every bone in his body he was taller.

"Ok, Cathy, you can go home," he said, still looking at Claire.

"You've got ten minutes," he said, turning on his heels, which Claire noticed with amusement were built up, and striding into his office, before sitting himself down in the huge leather chair behind the large dark wooden desk.

Claire and Wilson sauntered in, before easing themselves into the chairs set in front of the desk.

"We have 'got' as long as we need Mr. Woodward, unless you would prefer we conduct this at the station?"

"Try it, agent," he said, rolling her title around in his mouth as if it was something he had taken a bite out of and wished he hadn't. "My attorney will have that badge off you so quick you won't have time to get down on your knees and beg for forgiveness."

Claire, face impassive looked across at Wilson, who took it as his cue. He reached into his bag and retrieved a folder, before selecting two photographs, tenement blocks owned by Daniel Walsh and Tommy Jacobson. He placed them on the desk.

"Recognize those buildings, Mr. Woodward?" he said.

Claire knew it was a gamble. At this stage they had no idea which buildings Woodward and DPG were going after, but it was a fairly safe presumption that these two blocks would have been on his radar and, even if they weren't, one address on a spreadsheet looks pretty much like any other address. She did not expect someone like Samuel Woodward carried out many site inspections.

Woodward's eyes flicked to the photographs, then bored back into Wilson's.

"No. Your family home? Nice," he said.

Wilson read out the addresses. Claire studied Woodward's tanned face to see if there was any reaction, but there was nothing. Not even a flicker. She guessed in a job which was like being in a constant game of poker, with bluffs and counter bluffs, you wouldn't get very far if you showed your emotions on your face.

"We have it on good authority, Mr. Woodward, that DPG has been putting pressure, undue and no doubt illegal pressure, on landlords to sell. Landlords of blocks in the city exactly like these," Wilson said, his finger pressing down on the pictures. The tone of his voice showed he was losing patience with the stonewalling tactic of Woodward.

"I said you had ten minutes," Woodward said, leaning forward in his chair. "If you want to spend that time trying to give me a lesson on the machinations of the real estate market in this fine city, agent, then you are even more stupid than you look. I suggest you leave it to the people who are qualified in that area, stop wasting my time, and take your girlfriend here with you."

"We aren't here to talk about the real estate market Mr. Woodward, fascinating though that is," Claire said, stepping in before Wilson's anger overtook him and played into Woodward's hands. "We are here to talk to you about murder. Something we *do* know a lot about. Now, you have a decision to make. You either get down off that high horse you are pretending to ride and start cooperating or we will take you down to the station in cuffs, charge you for the murder of two males, and have a dozen of my colleagues here first thing tomorrow morning to go through every one of your accounts."

"I would also be surprised if the local TV networks didn't somehow get wind of what was going on and be here in numbers to film the whole thing."

She looked at him, her face deadpan, but inside she loved the way he seemed to deflate. Suddenly, the conversation, the power in the room, had flipped. The word murder had shaken him. Plus, the threat of federal agents going through his accounts was enough to make any VP quake in his boots. Even if he was squeaky clean, which Claire highly doubted, the stigma and publicity was something that few people, or even businesses could recover from.

It took him a couple of seconds, but Woodward made a physical effort to get his emotions and his mind back under control.

"I'm going to ignore the second part of that monologue, agent, but why the hell are you talking about murder?"

"Daniel Walsh and Tommy Jacobson," Wilson said. "Both landlords, both killed. When we did a little digging, we saw that landlords including Walsh and Jacobson, were coming under increasing pressure to sell. Now who do you think they were being pressured to sell to, Mr. Woodward? What we want to know is exactly what pressure that form took. Murder?"

Woodward swallowed. He was looking increasingly uncomfortable. It was amazing how the word murder did that to people. Claire guessed he was not used to being sideswiped in negotiations. Not used to not holding all the cards. She couldn't help but find the situation enjoyable.

"Do those names mean anything to you, Mr. Woodward?" Claire pressed.

She could see his brain working, weighing up whether to continue to bluff, play the arrogant high- flying executive, or to tell them what he knew. Or at least part of what he knew.

He blew out a breath. "Your math is screwed. It seems to me you've tried to put two and two together and come up with something that doesn't look like four. Or anything approaching it."

He was trying to come across as the confident, brash, arrogant vice president, but there were chinks in the façade now and Claire could see right through them. He was worried. She just needed to find out what about.

"Ok," she said, "we'll try a bit more math that hopefully we all understand. We, and when I say we, I mean the Federal Bureau of Investigation, and by logical extension, the United States government, needs you to do two things. First, you need to show us where you were on the dates when Daniel Walsh and Tommy Jacobson were killed. Second, you need to show us exactly what you have on both of those men, and the buildings they owned."

Wilson read out the dates and times. Woodward held his gaze for a couple of heartbeats then opened the leather-bound diary on his desk.

"Sorry to disappoint you, agent," he said, the old reassurance seeping back into his manner, "but I was in Detroit for the first date, and it was our AGM for the second one." He shut it with a thud and sat back, eyeing both agents, the trace of a smile on his lips.

"I would very much doubt a man in your position would be the one to… get his hands dirty. If I was being skeptical, I could possibly think the fact you have cast iron alibis for those dates was a little bit too convenient," Wilson said.

Woodward stared at the agent but said nothing.

"And the second part of my request?" Claire asked.

This time she was treated to a hard stare, but she stared back into his eyes, and it was the vice president of DPG who blinked first. He swung round to the large monitor on the right-hand side of his desk. After a few initial taps on the keyboard he swung the screen around so the agents could see.

Claire brought her chair nearer to the desk, leaning on the leather surface with her forearms. A bronze paperweight in the shape of a quill and pot of ink was in the way, so she gently pushed it aside. As soon as the skin of her fingers touched the cold metal, everything went black. Then blurry images started to form, but disappeared as soon as they gained any solid shape.

She desperately tried to focus on them, but they were gone, like snowflakes melting as soon as she grasped them.

What she could make out though was that every image, though different, had one thing in common. They were also not objects. They were numbers.

212.

Some were handwritten, others appeared to be the number on the side of a house. Others were on a spreadsheet.

All different. But all with that same number: 212.

Then she was back in the room, Samuel Woodward's PC screen in front of her. She quickly looked at Woodward and Wilson, but both men's gazes were intent on the screen.

She took a deep breath in to calm her racing heart, then focused once again on what was happening right in front of her.

"Daniel Walsh doesn't even own the building he leases out," Woodward said. "It's owned by a housing authority we are in discussions with. Walsh will know as much about those discussions as you two appear to."

The VP typed in the address of the second block, his eyes scanning the info that came up. A look of relief briefly flitted across his face before being replaced by one of satisfaction, bordering on smugness.

"As for Tommy Jacobson," he said, "he agreed to sell three weeks ago. Even with your grasp of business, you must understand it would make no sense for me or anyone at DPG to kill him."

Claire looked at the document on the screen. It did show that the sale was agreed earlier that month. She felt her cell phone vibrate in her pocket and pulled it out, looking at the caller ID.

"Agent King," she said turning around to face the door.

"Agent, we have just had a report of an abduction," the voice on the other end of the line told her, his voice urgent. "A woman this time. But her husband has told us she is a landlord of a tenement block."

CHAPTER TWELVE

Wilson slammed on the brakes after turning into the parking lot, bringing the car to a skidding halt. Claire leaped out and quickly took in the scene in front of her.

Blue flashing lights from an ambulance and three police cruisers gave the lot an added dramatic effect. To the side there was a knot of children, visibly distressed and being comforted by various adults, some in civilian dress, some in unform.

Away to the other side was another boy, distraught. A man, obviously his father, was crouched in front of him, his hands on his son's young shoulders, speaking to him, consoling him. Two officers, one male, one female, stood beside him.

Center stage however, and the sight that somehow was the most disturbing, was the minivan.

Half a dozen CSIs were standing behind it, one of whom was erecting a large floodlight on a tripod, its harsh white light shining into the rear of the minivan. Its doors were wide open.

The rest of the parking lot had been cordoned off, and as Claire looked, an officer was walking with a flashlight, the circle of light sweeping the asphalt in front of him. Looking, Claire guessed, for anything the victim, or the perp had dropped, scuff marks, tire tracks… anything.

Claire's mind went back to her conversation with Deputy Chief Flannagan. Perhaps her words had hit home. This had all the hallmarks of a third victim, or at least a third person taken. And this one was a woman. There was no way this would not make headlines especially with every news editor in the country desperate for more dirt for their reporters to find in this city.

She reminded herself that this was not as yet connected to the deaths of Daniel Walsh and Tommy Jacobson. The message may have become garbled in the scramble to get information. And it may also be a coincidence.

That was for them to find out.

The night air was cold, and Claire wished she had thought of bringing her coat from the hotel, but it had all been such a rush since they had touched down.

She stepped forward trying to see if there was a familiar face among the throng of activity but drew a blank. As she and Wilson walked towards the minivan, one of the CSI team noticed their approach.

She flashed her badge.

“Agent King, this is Agent Wilson.”

“Feds, what brings you here?” the man said. He was in his late twenties, with an accent straight out of the Texan songbook.

“We are in the city,” Claire said, matching his friendly tone of voice, “investigating two homicides. The preliminary information suggests this may be a third.”

“Preliminary information? What the hell is that? We only got here five minutes ago, and we’ve got diddly squat so far, agent.”

“We were told the lady who went missing is perhaps connected to our investigation,” Wilson said.

The man shrugged his shoulders. “Better speak to the uniforms.”

“Hey Tex, come here,” one of the man’s colleagues called, at least confirming her theory on the man’s place of birth.

“Duty calls,” he said and joined his team huddled around the trunk of the minivan.

Both agents’ heads turned to the group on their left. The father and son had been moved to a bench a little distance away, out of sight from the vehicle their wife and mother had apparently been taken from. A Black officer stood on his own talking into a cell phone. As Claire closed the distance, she could see he was a captain in the sheriff’s department.

“Captain,” she said after waiting for him to finish his call. “I’m agent Claire King; this is my partner Agent Mark Wilson. We are conducting an investigation into the homicides of Daniel Walsh and Tommy Jacobson.”

The captain looked at the agents with a mixture of suspicion and weariness, his grip tightening on the phone. "What's that got to do with this? We're dealing with a missing woman here."

"We were informed that the woman in question may have been connected to our case," Claire said calmly, not wanting to unnerve the man. Also not wanting to alarm any of the civilians present that this may be more than an abduction. “We’re just trying to gather any information that might be relevant.”

The captain took a deep breath, his eyes flicking from Claire to Wilson and back again. “I don’t know how much help I can be. We’re still trying to piece together what happened here.”

"Can you tell us anything?" Wilson spoke up, his voice soothing. "Any witnesses, any leads?"

The captain sighed, running a hand over his bald head. "All we know is that a woman disappeared from this parking lot."

"Who reported her missing?" Wilson asked.

"One of her friends," he looked around trying to locate the woman in person, but with the flashing lights, the darkness, and the amount of people milling around, it was impossible.

Claire was starting to find the slow drip of information coming from the captain frustrating.

"Look Captain, this is a live investigation. This woman is missing. If she is connected to our investigation, we have to find her. Soon. Sooner than soon. I know you and your men will be doing anything and everything to find her too, but *together* we are going to be in a helluva better position to find this woman. So, please can you tell us everything you know?"

The captain stared at her, and for a moment when he visibly bristled, she thought he was going to be a dead end. Then he gave another sigh, rubbed a hand over his head, and led them a few steps towards the grass park.

"Ok, agent," he began, failing to disguise the dislike for the word, "Jennifer Mannings brought her son to little league this afternoon. As far as we are aware, and her husband is aware," the captain indicated to the man with his boy at the bench, "it was just a normal afternoon. Mrs. Mannings helps out with the refreshments after the third innings. She went as usual to get the juice and what have you… and didn't come back. One of her friends came to see if she needed a hand and found the van doors open, but no Jennifer."

Claire looked across at the van. "Did she or anyone else see anything, anybody?" she asked.

"Nobody and nothing, agent. I guess we have to see what the old lab guys can find," he said his tone giving the impression he liked the CSI team as much as the FBI one.

"We were told that Mrs. Mannings is a landlord of some kind?" she asked.

The question seemed to throw the captain, and he looked at her as if she had just asked what the missing person's favorite movie was.

After a couple of heartbeats, he retrieved his notebook from his pocket and flicked to the right page.

"Yes," he said. Claire waited for him to elaborate but it quickly became obvious that there was nothing more forthcoming.

“Right, agents, I am in the middle of an investigation here. I have a woman to find,” and he strode off to two colleagues, one who was speaking animatedly into his cell phone.

“Unbelievable,” Wilson muttered.

“You wouldn’t think we are all on the same side, would you?” Claire said, before heading in the direction of the missing woman’s husband.

The young boy, still in his baseball uniform but with his dad’s jacket over his shoulders making him look like he had somehow shrunk, sat on the bench. He looked more lost than frightened, and Claire wondered exactly what he had been told. A woman police officer sat next to him. His father stood a couple of feet off in deep conversation with a male officer. He looked like he had been dropped into a world he hadn’t known existed until an hour ago. Like his son, he looked lost, but in addition to that he also looked terrified.

“Mr. Mannings?” Claire said, slowly stepping up to the man. He was in his early forties. A handsome face, that she guessed would be more handsome if it didn’t have the worries of the world written all across it. His brown hair was stuck up from his hands repeatedly pushing it up in anguish.

He whirled around to her, hope in his eyes. Hope that cut through her like a knife. She pushed aside the images in her mind of Tommy Jacobson and Daniel Walsh, dead, chained to radiators.

“Have you any news? Have you found her?” he said, his voice, his eyes pleading.

“Not yet Mr. Mannings, but you can rest assured that there are a lot of people, a lot of very good people, doing everything they possibly can *to* find her.”

Claire decided that unless absolutely necessary, she wouldn’t reveal who she and Wilson were, or why they were there and wanted to talk to him. Being told that his wife was very possibly the next victim of a serial killer wasn’t going to help his mood.

“I know you will have gone through everything already with some of my colleagues, but if you could answer a few more questions for me Mr. Mannings, it would really help us find Jennifer.”

He looked at her as if his mind was translating what she was saying into his own language.

“Of course. Anything. And call me Jack.”

“Ok Jack,” Claire said, leading him gently away from the other officers, and more importantly his son. “I just need you to fill in some gaps, from my point of view, in the picture we have of your wife. I understand she works in real estate?"

"Yes. Well, Jen is a landlord of a couple of blocks. Tenements, you know, not like condos or anything."

"Do you know if she has received any threats, from tenants, perhaps unhappy about the rent, or the state of the apartments, overdue repairs, anything?"

Jack shook his head, his face a mask of concern and confusion.

"No. Nothing. Why, do you think this has got something to do with Jen's work? Would someone kidnap her for that?"

"We don't know, Jack. We just need to look at your wife's situation from every possible angle," Claire said, hoping with every fiber in her body that the assumption the missing woman's husband had made about it being a kidnapping was correct. The logical side of her brain, the far bigger, stronger, more dominant side, thought that was very unlikely, however.

"Has she got her cell phone with her?" Wilson asked.

Again, the exasperated shake of Jack's head. "No. She left it on the bleachers in her bag. She was only going to be gone a few minutes. She was with friends..." He made a physical attempt to control his emotions which were in danger of running away.

"And you weren't here, Jack? When... this happened," Claire asked.

"No. I... I work in the city. I try to get off early when Josh is playing, at least to try and get to the last innings. I got here the same time as the first police cars arrived."

Claire considered the options. She was sure that whoever had taken Jennifer Mannings was the same person who had killed the other two landlords. That would give them another angle to attack with which to track down whoever was responsible. But, Jennifer had only been taken an hour and a half ago. There was still a very good chance she was still alive.

They couldn't afford to dig up and trawl through more information in an attempt to find out who had taken her. At least not until the worst came along, *if* it did come to that. Their number one priority right now was to do everything in their power to make sure it *didn't* come to that.

Claire reached out and put a comforting hand on Jack's shoulder, aware it was the same gesture that he had done with his son earlier.

"Thank you, Jack. And believe me, we will do everything humanly possible to find Jennifer and bring her safely back to you and your family."

There was a glimmer of hope in his eyes as he thanked Claire; then he looked across at Josh, his son, and that hope was quickly replaced by despair.

Claire walked off a safe distance and turned her back on the scene behind her before talking in hushed tones to Wilson.

"What do you think?"

He didn't say anything, but his expression said that he was thinking the exact same as her. That unless they managed to find Jennifer very quickly, she would be the third victim.

She walked quickly over to the minivan.

"Tex," she said to the backs of the three men studying the van's interior.

Tex turned round, something that looked like a ray gun gripped in his fist.

"Anything?" Claire asked, her voice urgent.

"Not as yet. Plenty of stuff to send to the lab but… my instincts tell me they won't turn up a whole lot of joy. But. We live in hope."

She nodded and looked at the back of the van. The overturned ice chest was the only sign of the struggle that had ensued here.

She turned around, eyes scanning for CCTV but finding none. Then seeing the sheriff's captain again, she jogged over. He was in conversation with his colleagues, but she placed a gentle hand on his elbow.

"Captain," she said, her voice urgent but hushed, not wanting it to carry to anyone else. "We have strong grounds to assume that Jennifer Mannings was taken by the same person who took and killed Daniel Walsh and Tommy Jacobson. If so, this is a potential homicide, not a kidnapping. The MO of this perp is to carry out the killing in basements, tenement block basements, after boarding up the windows. Deputy Chief Flannagan is already on the case with his men checking for recently refurbished basement windows. I strongly suggest you get every spare man you have to do the same. If we can find the window to the basement she is in, we have the best, probably the only chance of finding Jennifer Mannings alive."

The captain looked at her, the double impact of being told what to do by an FBI agent and the nature of the request not helping his decision making process.

"Just do it, Captain," she said, frustration finally getting the better of her.

"Come on, Wilson," she said, running back to the car.

Wilson had gunned the engine before his door was shut, reversing out of the parking lot at speed.

"Where to?" he said, slamming it into drive and hitting the gas.

"To check for newly boarded up windows. Every minute could be the difference between finding Jennifer alive or cutting her cold dead body from yet another radiator."

CHAPTER THIRTEEN

The streets were eerily quiet. The sound of sirens could be heard in the near distance, and every now and then a car raced by, the muffled sound of heavy drumbeats fighting with the six cylinders for sonic supremacy. But otherwise, the only noise was the laughter and catcalls of the groups of men huddled in the shadows and their own hurried footsteps.

It was cold now, the thin air being whipped down the streets on a stiffening breeze. But the dual actions of adrenaline and the focus of trying to find Jennifer Mannings still alive meant Claire barely noticed.

The two agents broke into a run, prompting a cheer from a group of young men outside a bail bond office. Claire didn't let her thoughts wander to the dangers of being on their own in this neighborhood at what was approaching midnight.

She could handle herself. She was armed. She had Wilson alongside her who ticked both those boxes too. But the whole place had a feeling of lawlessness, that the normal rules just didn't apply any more. These men on the corners of almost every block, they felt it too. They no longer skulked in the shadows.

The look in their eyes, those who were not too far gone on whatever drug of choice, was one of expectation. They believed that things were turning, changing, and they were going to be the ones who were suddenly on top.

But all of that was a sideshow. One that Claire could not afford to let distract her. Her number one priority, her *only* priority at this moment was to try to keep Jennifer Mannings alive. And the first step to achieving that was to find her!

Between the two of them, the sheriff's department, and Deputy Chief Flannagan, they had hastily split up the most likely neighborhoods. The different departments with their often opposing agendas and personalities were a constant cause of frustration, but at times like this, the unspoken element of competition did have its uses.

It was a larger area than Claire had imagined with more potential tenement blocks and basements where Jennifer could be held. But it was all they could do. The first block she and Wilson had gone to was covered in scaffolding. Renovation seemed to be going on of sorts, but it was all on the upper levels.

The second block on their list loomed up on the other side of the road, twenty yards to their left. Many of the roads in this particular neighborhood had been blocked, either by the police in an attempt to control movement, or by local gangs, using anything they could get their hands on to cordon off streets, better to control their territory.

This meant that they had made the decision to dump their vehicle and go on foot. Claire had forgotten the effect that altitude would have, and her head was feeling light, her lungs desperately sucking in air, by the time they reached the second block.

A handful of lights shone in the rooms on various floors, but most were in darkness.

Wilson, also panting heavily, shone his flashlight on the graffitied brickwork. The ground in front of them dropped down to a small walkway that circled the tenement block.

Claire quickly scoured the ground for a way down, but there didn't seem to be one within sight; so she slid down the ten feet, over a combination of broken bricks and rubble, landing with a jolt on the garbage littered pathway below. A second later, Wilson joined her, his feet catching on a clump of brick, sending him spinning into Claire, pinning her to the cold brick.

They stood there motionless like deer caught in headlights, holding onto each other, panting. Claire, her head resting on Wilson's broad chest felt his warmth, his reassuring presence a sudden oasis of comfort on this terrible night.

As if someone had flicked a switch, they both became aware of the situation, of the other's part in it at the same time, and pushed themselves apart. Claire was glad of the dark, meaning Wilson couldn't see the look on her face, the flush on her cheeks.

She cleared her throat and turned to face the building, her hand grasping for her flashlight.

Both solely focused on the matter at hand again, they shone their flashlights, the beams picking out the dark brick that rose up immediately in front of them. A steel door to their right was padlocked shut. There were no windows in view. The front of the building lay to their right, the pathway blocked by the entranceway to the front foyer. The two jogged along the narrow pathway, their feet crunching on beer cans and kicking glass bottles, their flashlights trained on the wall on their right.

Twenty yards along, the first window appeared. It was filthy but very much not boarded up. Claire felt her stomach tighten a notch, every failure feeling like Jennifer Mannings was slipping further away.

A minute later, the second window came into view. It was the same. Its cracked glass was covered in dust, even splashes of paint, but it had not been boarded up. There was also no light coming from the dark basement on the other side.

Just to make sure, they made their way as rapidly as they could along the rest of the passageway, but found nothing other than the same graffitied brickwork, and an abandoned grocery cart.

"Come on," Claire said, panting, refusing to let her spirits flag. "Next one."

They made their way up back to street level via a short flight of concrete steps.

Wilson, looking at the map on his cell phone, quickly reorientated himself. They studied the list. There were three more blocks on it. If they hadn't found Jennifer by then, nor heard from any of the other search parties… well, they would cross that bridge when and if they got to it.

Claire looked at the three remaining addresses. Her eyes stopped at the second one: 212 Aurora Drive. The vision came back to her, that number, 212 repeating over and over.

She pointed to it. "That one."

He glanced at her briefly, then punched it into his cell.

"One block. On the corner on the right," he said pointing down the dark street.

The pair set off at a sprint.

Halfway along, they were forced to make their way along the highway, which was largely empty, the sidewalk having been taken over by a crowd of twenty or more men, gathered around an impromptu bonfire and a speaker blaring out rap music. The men followed the two agents' progress but aside from some shouts, let them go unhindered.

The whole scene was surreal to Claire. It was like she had been parachuted into a nightmare, a computer game, or movie. Once again, she forced all extraneous thoughts from her head. She conjured up the image of Tommy Jacobson chained to the radiator. Of Jack comforting his son Josh.

Her legs ran faster, her arms pumped harder, her lungs sucked in ever greater gulps of the thin air.

The buildings on this block were even more rundown than the previous ones they had searched, with many of the windows boarded up and the graffiti more menacing. They turned the corner onto the next street, and the building they were looking for was in sight. It was a six-story brick building, with a sign hanging above the door that read "Cheap Rent."

A solitary light shone from a window on the top floor. Otherwise, it was in darkness. A car lot was on the opposite side of the street, razor wire fencing surrounding it. Two large dogs paced the practically empty grounds. One stopped, catching sight or scent of the two agents. It gave a loud bark, and then ran off to explore another, darker part of the yard.

Claire stopped in front of the block, gasping for breath. Her head was spinning, and she leaned on the wall, while her eyes scanned the façade. At all of the blocks they had visited so far they had been able to check for any basement windows from the outside. With this one, that would be impossible. Twenty-foot walls led off from both sides of the building. They may be able to get access from the back, but that would mean going another block on either side.

"Come on, we'll have to go in," she cried, leading the way to the double doors that sat above three brick steps.

Mercifully the doors were open. A square ante room faced them with an elevator in the middle, stairs leading up on the right, and another flight leading down to the left. The only light was from a fire exit sign, and they both flicked on their flashlights.

Walking quickly, they made their way to the stairway, which led down into darkness. After a right-angle turn, the way narrowed, a short stone corridor ending in a door.

From their flashlights they could see it was ajar.

The two looked at each other, both thinking the same thing. Claire drew her gun, slipped off the safety.

Using her elbow, she pushed the door further open and entered. The basement was dark, cold, and silent. Outside a siren screamed by.

"FBI officers," she called out, charging into the dark space, the light from her flashlight picking up details from the basement.

Her voice echoed around the large brick room, then died, leaving silence.

Her brain processed the images. Two large garbage dumpsters, a pile of doors stacked on top of each other, an aluminum sink unit next to them. Then the beam lit up a scene that made her heart stop.

A woman. Slumped against a radiator in the corner.

"Jennifer!" Claire cried, racing towards her, Wilson hot on her heels.

She knew she was dead before she knelt down and checked her pulse.

No living person would be at that angle, their head lolling back, their arm twisted behind their back.

Leaving her with the body, Wilson quickly skirted the room, checking to see if whoever had done this was still there, but they both knew they were too late. That they had missed him.

Claire put her gun away, replacing it with her cell phone. A leaden, sick feeling had replaced the adrenaline of earlier. Her eyes on Jennifer's lifeless face and body, she called in what they had found.

"This has been boarded up. Fresh screws," Wilson called from the other side of the basement, his flashlight trained on the window in front of him.

Claire looked over, trying to orientate herself to the street outside.

"I'm not even sure that would have been visible from the street," she said, standing up.

She turned her attention back to the body at her feet. Her mind going out to Jack, the husband, who would be waiting desperately to hear news, positive news of his wife's safe return. To Josh, the young boy who only went out to play baseball with his buddies.

Anger rose up inside of her, and an even greater determination to find the monster who had done this.

She looked down at Jennifer Mannings's face, studying her features for the first time. Something on her pale, almost blue lips made her stop.

She peered closer, shining her flashlight onto the face.

On her lips were two or three metal shavings, the same as they had found in the mouths of the previous two victims.

"Wilson!" she called. "Look at this."

She waited for her partner to run over before parting the dead woman's lips with the end of her pen.

The inside lips, gums, and tongue were coated with the same metal shavings.

Claire and Wilson exchanged a look.

She stood up, suddenly not wanting to be so close to the dead woman. Her knees, stiff from crouching, tired from the long day and the high-altitude exercise gave slightly and she fell onto the cold cast iron of the radiator.

The awful basement, Jennifer Mannings's place of death, vanished.

Suddenly she was in a hospital ward, a metal framed bed in front of her. On the bed, dressed in stripey white and blue pajamas, was a small boy. He was weeping uncontrollably, his face a picture of misery, wrought with a despair that someone that young should never have to experience.

She was drawn to the boy but couldn't move, could only observe, her heart ripped apart by his suffering.

Then, as suddenly as it had appeared, the vision blinked out, and she was back in the basement, Jennifer Mannings's dead body below her.

"Claire?" Wilson said, reaching out and steadying her.

Suddenly there was the sound of heavy footsteps on the stairway, and three men entered the basement, their flashlights momentarily blinding them.

***

Claire stared at the beer in front of her. The image of the boy haunted her thoughts, as did the face of Jennifer Mannings. She wondered how close to saving her life, how close they had been to catching the killer. The three officers who had joined them shortly after she and Wilson had entered the basement - had they made decisions that, had they gone another way, meant they would have arrived in time?

She looked up, took in her surroundings. The hotel bar was like every other hotel bar in America. It served a purpose. A purpose mainly for people to while away the hours, to forget the day they had just endured, or put off the one that was coming.

Claire's mind was a cacophony of thoughts and emotions. As well as the case, the exhaustion of the day, everything else that was happening, a new one was trying to make itself known.

It wasn't a new one, if she was completely honest with herself. It had been there for a while, but it was getting stronger, pushing its way further and further to the front of her consciousness. Now that she was in comforting surroundings, the soothing buzz of the alcohol seeping into her, that feeling was getting harder to ignore.

She looked across at Wilson.

"You're quiet," he said, catching her eye. "The altitude takes it out of ya, doesn't it?"

She nodded her assent, and took a sip of her beer.

"Tomorrow we'll see if forensics found anything from either of the Jennifer Mannings crime scenes," he said, and Claire got the impression he was simply filling the silence.

"The coroner's got to prioritize this now. When we find out exactly what those shavings are, how they fit into all of this, that is the way into this case," he said, downing his beer to emphasize the point. "Same again?" he asked.

"Yeah, go on, but then I'm hitting the hay. I'm beat," she said and watched him call over the waitress.

Claire looked at Wilson. Despite herself, despite every professional bone in her body, despite every instinct, she couldn't deny the feelings that she was starting to have for the man. Feelings that were becoming harder and harder to ignore.

She had told herself to get a grip. She wasn't a teenager. She had a job to do, a job where people's lives were at stake.

She knew all that.

But she also knew that unless she confronted those feelings, they would only get stronger and she would only get more confused, less able to do that job.

The waitress set the beers down, and Claire drained the last of her glass.

She took a deep breath.

"Wilson… Mark…"

He looked at her; a smile stretched across his features, then faded. He took a sip of his beer, and she could tell he was suddenly as nervous as she was. Did he know what she was about to say. Or about to try and say?

"I don't know how to say this, and I don't know even if I *should* say this, but what I have learned in my thirty-two years is that ignoring something doesn't make it go away. And…" she took a sip of her beer, "I don't think I want it to go away."

Wilson was looking more and more uncomfortable. Half his beer had already disappeared down his throat, and his fingers were picking at the label on the bottle as if they were trying to get to a secret message beneath.

She felt like she had leapt off a cliff. There was no going back even if she wanted to.

"I know this is the last thing you want to hear, especially now, in the middle of everything that is going on, but I think I like you, Mark. No, I'm pretty certain I like you. And I don't mean just as a partner. A work partner."

As she was saying the words, hearing her voice, it sounded like she was listening to someone else. An awkward girl, trying to get across her most intimate feelings but failing horribly. How could she be so adept at dealing with everyone else, but so awful at dealing with her own feelings, emotions, and desires?

She forced herself to look into Wilson's eyes, who, with what looked like an equally impressive effort, did the same. He looked like he wanted to be anywhere at that moment but at that table in that bar.

Her heart didn't know whether to race or stop in its tracks and did a stuttering flutter somewhere in between. She wanted the ground to open up and swallow her. How could she have misjudged this whole thing so badly?

"No, Claire," Wilson said, his voice strange, taut, "that is not the last thing I want to hear. Far from it…I…" he seemed to be groping for the right words, and took a swig from his beer, perhaps hoping they were to be found in the amber liquid.

Claire's cell phone on the table in front of her suddenly rang, making them both jump. They looked at it, both seeing it as an escape.

The word 'Dad' was displayed on the screen.

She closed her eyes, feeling sick for a completely different reason now.

"I have to take this," she said, her hand reaching for the phone.

CHAPTER FOURTEEN

"Claire, it's your father." The words came out of the tiny speaker clutched in her hand. As always, they brought with it the tenseness in her stomach. The nauseous, spinning out of control sensation, one that pitched her back to being a frightened child. Which was exactly what she *had* been, mentally at least, all those years ago.

And then, on the tail of all those emotions came the anger. With him for causing her to feel like that whenever he could be bothered to pick up the phone. And with herself for allowing this man to still have such an effect upon her.

"I'm just getting in the elevator," she said, trying to keep her voice flat, emotion-free, and just about succeeding. "I'll call you in three minutes." She shut the call off before he could reply, then hit the call button on the rank of elevators. She needed those three minutes to compose herself.

Briefly she imagined the scene behind her, back in the bar. Wilson's eyes following her into the foyer, her stupid schoolgirl confession ringing in his ears. But his response…

The door to the elevator on the far right swished open. A young couple, laughing and holding hands, exited, and Claire replaced them, stepping into the small space that was filled with the pungent cocktail of the couple's aftershave and perfume.

The security of her room didn't have the calming effect she had hoped, but before she could allow herself to delay or even worse, to abandon for the night what she knew she had to do, she brought up the last number received on her cell phone and hit return call.

"That was more like four minutes," the gruff voice answered.

If it had been anyone else in the world, perhaps with the exception of the Chief, Claire would have assumed he had been joking. With her father she was pretty damn sure he wasn't and had instantly reverted to any tiny chance to criticize her. At least he sounded sober.

"So, what progress have you made? Have you got the proper people working on Donna's case?"

There was that steel grip on her stomach again. She forced herself not to jump down the phone at the dig. At the assumption that the team that could be labeled the 'proper people' working at the FBI didn't include among their number his only daughter.

She also reassessed her opinion of his sobriety. He may not have been incoherent, but he was probably halfway there.

"Yes, I've sent all the details. It isn't going to be quick, but we are reopening the case…"

"It should never have been closed. The killer is still out there. While my Donna is six feet in the earth," the angry, bitter voice forced Claire to sit on the bed.

She closed her eyes, calmed her breathing. Every instinct was to answer back, to fight her case, but she knew exactly where that would lead, and it wasn't a place she wanted to go, especially as she had taken the first tentative steps towards redemption.

"It's a turn of phrase, Father. It will have the best detectives in the country, some of the best minds at the agency, my own included," she couldn't stop herself from adding, "looking into this case. Every aspect. Things have changed since then. A lot of advances have been made in those twenty years."

"I need you to find who did this to her. To me."

Claire could hear her father take a deep slug of a drink that she knew would not be anything less than forty percent proof.

"I need you to do it to fix me," he said, his voice tailing off into self-pity.

Claire waited, her ears straining to see if he would finish the sentence with 'to fix us' but there was just the sound of another gulp of liquor.

For the thousandth time she felt the urge to scream, "She was my mother! You weren't the only one who lost someone," but once again she held her tongue, pushed the emotion and anger down, where it had good company with all the other emotions swirling around inside her after that terrible day.

"Leave it with me; I'll call as soon as I hear anything," she heard herself saying before ending the call.

She sat in silence on the bed.

Her mind was a maelstrom of emotions, none of them good. It was hard enough in the middle of a case, to get your head straight, to be able to clear the rest of the noise and focus on the elements that would crack it.

The case itself was complex enough, with the backdrop of social unrest that may or may not be the cause or catalyst for the killer's actions.

On top of that was this business with her father. The case of her murdered mother. The specter of the Artist was never far from Claire's thoughts either. How, when he had so nearly ended her life so recently, was in all likelihood still at large.

And then the icing on the cake was the scene in the bar downstairs earlier.

Little wonder she thought her head was about to explode, and that was without all the uncertainty of the visions and her own mental health.

She picked up her cell phone and sought out the name who had always helped her when things got too tough, too unbearable, or just too damn confusing.

Bernadette.

Her mentor. The person who had put her where she was today. The person who had made sure she had survived everything that had gone on since getting there.

The only person in her life for the past decade or so who had been anything like a parent figure for her, despite their relationship starting out when she had been her lecturer at university.

"Hi, are you awake?" she texted.

Almost immediately the reply popped up on the screen. "Yes. Everything okay, honey? Need a chat?"

Claire was about to reply in the affirmative when she just hit call instead.

"Hey Claire, is everything ok?" the familiar voice asked, and already Claire felt calmer.

"Yes. No," she replied.

It was twenty minutes later when she ended the call. She felt better, simply talking things through. She hadn't gone into the case, just the fact she was in Denver, with the added difficulties that was causing. Most of the time had been taken with going over the issue with her father, one that Bernadette was very aware of, and had been throughout their time together as lecturer/student and then friends.

As always, Bernadette had alleviated the guilt that Claire felt about her feelings towards her father, and the fact she had dragged her feet for so long. Bernadette had flipped it on its head, made her feel good about the steps she had made, and made her feel justified in how she was dealing personally with her relationship with her father.

At the same time, she had the knack of not pushing the blame onto her father. As always, Claire came off the call with Bernadette feeling so much better, so grateful, but also desperate to be able to repay the ever mounting debt that she felt she owed her friend, despite knowing that Bernadette would never see it that way.

The one thing she had not mentioned was what had happened downstairs with Wilson, and the feelings that she was starting to feel for her partner. She vaguely wondered why she had failed to mention it. Fear of coming across as a lovesick teenager? Embarrassment at being so out of control of her feelings as a supposedly mature and successful, intelligent adult?

Thoughts of Wilson made her wonder where he was. Was he still at the bar, drowning his own confusion and embarrassment with beer, or had he retired to his room, not having given the incident another thought?

She tentatively grappled with the idea of texting him, to try and determine the lay of the land, but quickly rejected that. She would only make a bad situation worse. Only serve to dig the hole she had dug a little deeper.

She would have to deal with it tomorrow.

Wearily, she undressed and crawled into bed, covering her head with the thin sheet, fully aware that she was mirroring her actions as a young girl, in an attempt to keep the outside world at bay.

Despite her exhaustion, it was an hour before she fell into a fitful sleep, the black oblivion of the night and unconsciousness broken by the alternate images of an angry screaming man, raging at her and the world, and the terrified child, whimpering alone on the hospital bed.

CHAPTER FIFTEEN

Claire's eyes widened when she saw that the coroner's report had come back.

She sat up in bed, noting the time when the confidential email was sent had been 5:38am. She reassessed her opinion of the department slightly but put their new found work ethic and interest in the case down to pressure from above as opposed to a complete change of mentality. Still it was good news, or, she hoped, it was at least *some* news, as she sat up in bed and opened the file.

Her eyes scanned down the first report, the one for Daniel Walsh. Near the end was the bit she had been looking for. One word jumped out from the screen.

Lead.

The metal shavings in the victim's mouth were lead.

She thought for a few seconds, her brain digesting this information, before she quickly opened the other report, the one for Tommy Jacobson. As she had known it would, that showed the same. Both victims had been found with lead shavings in their mouths, and it was a certainty that the analysis of those in Jennifer Mannings's mouth would come back the same.

She texted Wilson, saying the reports had come back and that the metal had been lead and that she would be downstairs in twenty minutes, glad that they had something to focus on.

The foyer was surprisingly busy for the fact that it was barely seven o'clock. Claire, her hair still damp from the shower, watched the people going about their everyday lives. Each with their own worries and issues. She doubted if any had the added concern of trying to find the person who was loose in the city chaining landlords to radiators and putting lead shavings into their mouths.

Her thoughts were broken by the sight of Wilson walking through the revolving doors, a tray of coffees and bagels held aloft.

Claire forced herself to make eye contact and smile, her fear that her body would betray her and blush not coming to fruition.

"You're a lifesaver," she said, taking the proffered drink and food. There was a pause, and Claire could sense the huge elephant in the room. She could pretend it wasn't there, but she knew full well that it would follow the pair of them around all day. All week, and for the rest of their working relationship. Now was not the time to allow stupid personal issues to derail a life and death case.

"Look, Wilson, about last night. I… we were both tired, maybe a little emotional. Let's park whatever we said, whatever we were going to say for another time. For after we have the maniac who is committing these homicides."

Wilson looked like a drowning man who had been handed a life raft. He nodded, took a swig of his too hot coffee, winced, then changed the subject. "Lead? Did the reports say anything else?"

"No, nothing that I could see would be of any help. I'll forward them on. Let's walk to the precinct; it's only two blocks and I could do with the fresh air, no matter how thin and oxygen starved it is."

Outside, the sidewalk was in shadow, the sun yet to rise up over the tops of the surrounding buildings, but the coolness was refreshing.

"The toxicology reports show that the cause of death was lead poisoning," Claire said over a mouthful of ham and cream cheese bagel.

"The cause of death?" Wilson stopped and stared at his partner, forcing her to do the same.

"I assumed it was some form of symbolism or token the killer had left to signify something," he said, incredulity written on his features, "not the actual means of killing them. Wow. I thought lead poisoning was something that took place over years. Trace amounts building up in your body…"

"Yes that's usually how it comes about, but Daniel Walsh, Tommy Jacobson, and I expect Jennifer Mannings, not only had lead shavings in their mouths but had substantial amounts in their stomachs and digestive systems. They had ingested decades' worth of lead."

"Wow," Wilson said again, setting off again, slowly in the direction of the precinct. "What a way to go."

"Horrible though it is, there has to be a reason why someone has chosen that method to kill his victims. It is hardly the most straightforward, or I would have thought, the most guaranteed way of carrying out a homicide. It *has* to be linked to why he has chosen the three people he has, and why he has chosen to kill them," Claire said.

They had reached the corner of the block, the sun shining out of a pure blue sky casting shadows of their figures over the sidewalk and cycle lane.

Claire put the last of her bagel into her mouth and chewed thoughtfully. This was more like it. Last night, due to a combination of circumstances, she had felt hemmed in by problems on all sides. Now she had been given a ladder.

Something to get her teeth into, a puzzle that could be solved.

Wilson watched her, waiting for her to speak. He knew his partner well enough to know that when she was quiet, she was thinking.

"There's something else," she said, swallowing the last of the bagel. "Something that's been nagging at me since yesterday."

"What's that?" Wilson asked.

"The killer is targeting landlords, right?" Claire said, looking at Wilson. "But why landlords? Why not anyone else?"

Wilson shrugged. "Maybe he has a grudge against landlords. Maybe he's been evicted before or his parents have, perhaps."

Claire shook her head. "I don't think it's that simple. There has to be something more specific. What you're describing leads to what Jonny Cairns did. It makes people angry; they lash out at that particular landlord. They don't go after the whole profession."

They crossed the junction, and on reaching the other side, it was Claire's turn to stop. She pulled her partner to the side, away from a group of suited businessmen making their way in the opposite direction.

"There's something else I should tell you. It may or not be… relevant I guess."

She looked at him, hoping he would jump to the right conclusion, and fill in the gap. She wasn't disappointed.

"This is about your visions? Have you had another one Claire?"

She could actually detect excitement in his voice and manner. The skepticism had all but gone. Her heart soared. She had felt that what she had been going through with her visions was a burden she carried alone. It was something that would always come between her and everyone else, certainly everyone else in her department.

She knew Wilson wasn't all the way onboard yet, but he was a lot closer. Even having one person she could talk to normally about them was a huge weight off her mind.

She nodded. "Two actually." She took a deep breath. Despite her relief at Wilson's seeming acceptance, it was still something she felt uneasy talking about. Having spent her whole life dealing with facts and evidence, and even heartfelt instincts, she found it awkward to talk about something so strange, so mystical even, in the same tones.

"The first was in Woodward's office. It was very brief. Odd. Just the number 212, over and over. Not a sign, as in one sign with the number, just dozens of different ways it was written, each for a second, no more, always the same, 212."

Wilson screwed his eyes, as if trying to recall why that had relevance, then it came to him.

"The building Jennifer Mannings was found in. That was 212. You chose that over the buildings we had on our list."

Claire nodded, but unenthusiastically. "And a lot of good that did us. Jennifer was already dead when we got there…" She looked across the highway, at a police cruiser pulling up at a stoplight. "And that may have been a coincidence. I don't know. But there was another one…"

"In the basement, where Jennifer Mannings was found. I remember," he said, "what with everything else I didn't get a chance to ask you about it. What did you see?"

Claire closed her eyes, trying to conjure up the image as accurately as she could.

"It was of a child," she said, "a boy. I would guess he was five or six. He was in a hospital ward. On a bed. He was… he was so, so unhappy. He was crying, weeping. I could see him, but couldn't reach out. I could feel his misery. It was… it was awful."

Wilson reached out and laid his hand on her shoulder. A natural, comforting gesture.

"Anything else?" he asked, his voice gentle.

Claire scrunched her face up in concentration.

"I… I don't think so. The boy, he was dressed in these blue and white stripey pjs; they looked too big for him. The bed was, well just a hospital bed…"

"Was there anyone else in the ward? Any sounds?" he urged.

Claire shook her head in frustration. "No. Just the sound of him crying. Whimpering. The rest of the ward… it's like it is out of focus… it's hard to explain, it's like your eyes can only focus on one part of the picture."

She looked at Wilson, who was clicking his fingers, his own face scrunched up now.

"What is it?" she asked.

"I… I don't know. Something you said…" He tapped his hands on the side of his forehead, willing the half-remembered thought to the surface.

"The pjs!" he exclaimed, a look of triumph on his face. "The blue and white stripey pjs."

Claire watched her partner's face. He had recalled the detail that had hooked him; now she watched as he tried to work out what, if any, relevance it had to their case.

"My ex-girlfriend, my first serious girlfriend when I knew what serious meant, was a nurse. In a hospital." His speech was staccato, as he worked it out as he was saying it, not sure himself where he was going. "She… she worked in pediatrics. So did her mom. They used to talk about how all the kids there, on the wards, used to be given these same blue and white stripey pjs. It was like a uniform for the ward. I think it was meant to just be for the poorer kids, those who came in with only their diapers or whatever… but they rolled it out to everyone so that everyone looked the same."

Claire nodded and waited. Her initial enthusiasm waning as she struggled to see how this could help them.

"Do you think it was specific to your ex's hospital?" she asked hopefully.

Wilson shook his head. "Nah, it was countrywide as far as I can remember. They used to joke about it."

Claire sighed in frustration, and Wilson picked up on it.

"But that isn't it," he said quickly. "Before my ex started working at the ward, just before, the government, or some group of bean counters on some committee deemed that they should be done away with. Replaced by gowns, I think. I remember her mom brought several home to be used by her cousins, that's why it stuck in my memory."

Claire quickly processed this new information. "When would that have been?"

Wilson pursed his lips, "Let me see." He looked up into the cloudless sky, running through the mental arithmetic in his head. "It must be twenty years since they stopped using them on the wards, maybe a couple of years more. I'm sure we can check."

Claire nodded, excited once more. "This puts a different perspective on it all. The boy in my vision, he would be at least in his mid-twenties now." She paced around in a circle, her head nodding, her brain clutching new information, filtering it, keeping some, discarding others.

She stopped mid rotation and stared at Wilson. "The boy is not a victim. He is… was the killer." She clasped her hands to her temple, ignoring the puzzled looks of a man walking by. "Come on, Claire, think, think," she said to herself. "Why is that important? How does that fit in with what else we know? The lead poisoning. The landlords. The misery of this young boy who would go on to commit these horrible crimes."

“The lead poisoning!” both agents said at once.

“That has to be it,” Claire cried. “The boy I saw, the boy who would turn into the killer must have lost someone close. His parent, or parents, due to lead poisoning. It was prevalent in poorly managed tenement blocks. That’s why he is going after landlords, and not just any landlords, but ones of exactly the same type of building where he grew up. The types that had killed – in his mind anyway – his parents, or whoever he had lost. A sibling maybe.”

She looked at Wilson, her eyes imploring him to agree.

He nodded, at first slowly, then more and more assuredly.

“It may be a stretch, we may have cut a few corners, filled in the odd gap here and there, but that *has* to be what this case is all about!” Claire said, certain she was in the right ballpark.

They both turned towards the precinct and hurried the final block there.

“All we have to do,“ Claire said, finding the effort of walking briskly and talking excitedly was leaving her short of breath, “is find someone in the area who lost someone close due to lead poisoning twenty or so years ago.”

“Or,” Wilson said, holding his finger up in the air as he strode beside his partner, “someone who suffered from lead poisoning themselves. It may have ruined their life directly.”

Claire quickly considered that, then nodded her consent. “Yes, and then,” she said turning her face to Wilson, “we have our man!”

CHAPTER SIXTEEN

The lead poisoning wormhole Claire and Wilson had burrowed into was larger and more labyrinthine than they could have imagined. The picture postcard view out the window of their shared office just shone a darker light on the facts, figures, lies, and injustices that scrolled on and on down their laptop screens.

Claire forced herself to remain focused on the task at hand. Their number one, and only objective, namely, to find out the monster that had killed those three people. They were FBI agents. The deeper social issues and injustices were a job for the politicians, the judges, the regulatory bodies. When those started sticking their noses into to *her* field of expertise, it not only made her hackles rise but severely lessened her ability to do her job.

It would be hypocritical and counterproductive in every possible way if she allowed herself to be distracted from this case, for doing the exact same thing.

She and Wilson had been excited when they had rushed back to the precinct, both suddenly seeing the case opening up in front of them. Their plan had been simple. Look for anyone who between twenty and thirty years ago had lost someone due to lead poisoning, or who had suffered themselves. If that didn't work, they would push the envelope back another decade. And so on.

Wilson's memory had been more or less spot on. One phone call had confirmed that the blue and white stripey pjs had been withdrawn almost exactly twenty years ago.

"You thinking what I'm thinking?" Wilson said, looking over his laptop to Claire.

"That this is just the tip of an iceberg? Yep," she replied, sensing in her partner the same frustrations that were dawning on her.

"We came here initially to solve two homicides," he said rising from his chair and going to the window, leaning his back against the ledge. "Not routine homicides I grant you, but still, two dead bodies. What we find is a city on the edge of a civil war, that may or may not have been manufactured by some rogue banking group in order to drive prices down and empty whole districts. Conveniently the very same districts that they are trying to buy up."

"Then we discover that the killer's chosen MO is lead. Scratch a little below the surface and there's something like a half million deaths from lead poisoning nationwide. Thousands, perhaps tens of thousands in Denver." He looked at his partner, his face a mask of disbelief.

"You are right Wilson. But," she said, pushing her chair away from the desk, and repeating the same mantra she had told herself, "that is not our job. Our job is to find the person who tied those three innocent people to a radiator and forced them to ingest massive quantities of poison. Everything you have just said makes that task a whole lot harder, but it doesn't take away from the fact that it's why we are in this city, that is what we will do, and then we will leave."

"We may not agree with it, we may not like it, but it is what we are going to do." She looked at her partner, holding his eyes for a couple of beats. Then he nodded and turned to face the window.

"I know." He sighed, his knuckles rapping the cool glass. "I think I walked in here thinking we were going to pull up a list of half a dozen names and the perp would jump out. We'd find him, slap the cuffs on him. Job done, and we could leave this powder keg of a city."

Despite herself, Claire smiled.

"When is it ever that simple? When is our job ever that simple?" she asked.

Wilson turned to face her, a smile on his face, albeit a resigned one. "True. That's why they pay us millions of bucks a year to do it."

Claire's smile morphed into a full-blown laugh. "I'm glad the Chief followed up on my recommendation for your raise then."

Her face became serious again, and her eyes returned to her screen.

"I think we do need a different strategy though." She tapped her fingers against the desk, weighing options, then went for the simplest. "You go through the hospital lists, picking out anyone who ticks the boxes, then I'll filter out the ones who could conceivably chain three adults, two of them men, to a radiator and force-feed them lead. If you get snow blind we can swap. Deal?"

"Deal," he said, striding back to his desk.

A little over an hour later, two lists sat beside Claire King's laptop. One long one, with every name but one crossed out, and one short one. A very short one. It contained one name, the same name that stood out on the other list as not having a black ink line running through it.

The names had come thick and fast from Wilson. Many were easy to discount. They had either died or moved out of the state, or even out of the country. Others were too old, too infirm, or, after a little bit of digging, were just not the people who would or could do what this person had done.

Claire wasn't merely looking for felons with rap sheets as long as her black cotton clad legs, but they couldn't waste time chasing around the city, interviewing everyone from the list. Even with substantial police help, that would take weeks, months even. She dreaded to think how big the body count would be by then. And with everything else going on in the city, she would hardly describe the help the police were able to provide as substantial. If you could describe it as help at all.

There was also something else that had become apparent. Something that they would perhaps have to face at a later point but at this moment, just had to ignore.

The lists of names available to Wilson, extensive though they were, were not complete. Far from it. For multiple reasons, people had slipped through the system, or had never even been on it.

There was another elephant in the room. One Claire realized with a little embarrassment that had company. Wilson was only looking at men. That showed a level of faith in her vision of the small boy in a hospital that even she was not sure she held.

Wilson sent over another five names, each was added to the long list.

Claire set about digging up what she could on each one. Hoping at least one would be transferred to the shorter list.

The first two were dead. The third looked promising. He had lost his stepmother to lead poisoning twenty-five years ago. He had been in and out of institutions before seemingly turning his life round and becoming a relatively successful cage fighter on the local circuit. Claire was picturing him chaining Daniel Walsh to the radiator, forcing him to drink the deadly concoction, when her eyes alighted on the next page of his record. He was in the state penitentiary, serving fifteen years for his part in a drive-by shooting thirteen months ago.

So much for turning his life around. So much for being the man who killed Daniel Walsh and the other two landlords.

The other two names proved just as fruitless. One was a mayor in a city forty miles away. The other was a professor of environmental studies in Barcelona.

"Finished," Wilson declared, pushing himself away from the desk, yawning and rubbing his eyes with his balled up fists, in a way that made him look oddly childlike. "How many have we got?"

"One," Claire said.

"One?" Wilson stood up, coming round to Claire's side of the desk. "Is that good or bad?"

"I guess that depends if Danny Sabatini is our man. Every indication suggests that he very well could be, so I think it could be a good thing. Maybe our luck is changing."

The two peered at Claire's screen as she brought up more and more details about Danny Sabatini.

"Thirty-five years old," Claire said, picking out the relevant parts from the long list of information. "Was first admitted to a hospital… twenty-seven years ago for suspected lead poisoning from a faulty water main…" the couple looked at each other. Her pulse was beating faster. "He's been in and out of hospitals and clinics since then. Seems to have suffered physical and mental issues caused by the lead."

"The mental effects could explain the MO," Wilson said, his hands resting on the back of Claire's chair, his face level with hers.

"Has been convicted of a string of crimes, many involving violence, or at least the threat of it… appears to have been treated leniently, probably down to his mental issues… anger management and counseling sessions…"

"Nothing for the last five years. Turned over a new leaf, or building up for the big one?" Wilson asked. "My money's on the second of those options."

"It seems he hasn't worked for the last three and a half years," Claire said, pointing to a list of dates on the screen.

"Retired at thirty-five, not bad," Wilson replied.

Claire read out the address. "It doesn't sound like a tenement block." She quickly plugged it into Google Maps.

"Phew…" Wilson said pursing his lips, "that's at the other end of the spectrum to a tenement block. Look at the size of some of the properties on that street."

"Not only that," Claire scrolled up and to the left a little on the map, her index finger pointing to an area of green. "That is the park where Jennifer Mannings was abducted."

CHAPTER SEVENTEEN

"What do you want?" The question was thick with hidden meaning.

Claire looked at the woman peering out at her. She had opened the door just two inches, the length of the chain that fixed the heavy white wooden door to the equally heavy white wooden doorframe.

"I am looking for Danny Sabatini, is he here?" Claire repeated.

The woman blinked, and though she couldn't see it, she got the sense that she also swallowed.

"I am with the FBI ma'am; I urgently need to speak with Mr. Sabatini. Now, is he at these premises?" Her voice rose with frustration.

The drive over to the house had confirmed both Claire and Wilson's assumption about the area. It was affluent. A world away from the squalid tenement blocks and neighborhoods that had formed the backdrop to much of their investigation. The house of Danny Sabatini was certainly not the grandest they had passed, and was one of the smallest on the street, but it was still the sort of property Claire doubted she would ever be able to afford.

They had parked on the street, Claire walking up the sloping drive, while Wilson slipped away to the side of the house, making sure Sabatini didn't escape out the back.

She hadn't drawn her gun, though her hand was inside her black jacket and she could feel its reassuring cool metal on her fingers. The house may be worth ten times or more than that of Jonny Cairns, but it didn't mean she was in any less danger.

Sabatini had shown he was capable of sickening acts. He would be a desperate man. She had not been faced with a gun in her face, but her thudding heart and alert senses were proof that this was still a tense situation.

The face of the woman stared out at her, her eyes darting from Claire to the empty drive behind her, and back to the agent. She seemed frightened, and Claire wondered if she was being held against her will, held hostage by Sabatini.

Claire's eyes tried to look beyond the figure, but the gap was narrow and the small sliver of light it let in didn't penetrate the gloom behind.

"What do you want?" the woman asked again. Her voice was tense, but Claire thought it was perhaps nerves not terror that was causing it.

With an effort, Claire kept her patience, which was threatening to run away, in check.

She held her card up to the gap, using it as an excuse to get closer, to try and look beyond the section of the face that was almost wedged in the gap.

The woman's eyes went to the card, but Claire could tell she wasn't reading it. She seemed to be stalling for time, desperately trying to think of some way to deal with the situation but failing miserably.

Suddenly Claire sensed movement behind the woman, and her hands gripped the gun at her shoulder. Then another section of face appeared, above the woman's. The two faces peering out would have been comical in any other situation, but Claire felt no instinct to laugh.

Even with the small section of the face visible to her, she knew the man at the door was not Danny Sabatini. The hair was too light. The features too angular.

"I am with the FBI. I am here to speak to Danny Sabatini. I need to see Mr. Sabatini urgently. Now, is he here?" Claire said, her voice urgent.

Both heads withdrew, and for a second Claire thought the door was about to be shut in her face and she was poised to throw herself at it.

But then the chain was withdrawn, and the door was opened a fraction more. The woman had withdrawn a foot behind, and the man now stood in front of her, holding the door with his hand, keeping the gap just wide enough for his whole head to poke through.

Like the woman's before him, his eyes flicked nervously from Claire to the driveway, and then beyond to their parked car on the street below. They returned to Claire.

"He is sick," the man said. Claire could hear the woman pacing behind the man.

Claire wondered if this *was* a delaying tactic, and they were giving Sabatini the opportunity to escape out the back. If that was the case, he would find Wilson would have something to say about that. She kept her ears honed for the telltale sounds of a struggle reaching her from the rear of the property.

As of yet, it was all silent.

"I understand he is sick, but I still need to see him. Mr. …? Are you related to Danny Sabatini?"

The head withdrew slightly and there was a whispered conversation between the man and the woman. Then the head reappeared.

"He is too ill to see anyone. Doctor's orders," he said. Again, his eyes flitted between Claire and the driveway. He swallowed and licked his lips, his body swaying slightly as he stepped from foot to foot. His hand rearranged itself on the door.

"I am going to count to three, and if you don't let me in and tell me who you are I will arrest you for obstructing the efforts of a federal agent. One."

"He is my brother-in-law. I'm not related by blood. He is here but he is dying. The doctor said that he should not be put under any stress. That he should not see anybody or it will… it will kill him." The words came out in a torrent.

Claire looked at the man. He was clearly very nervous about something. He was also not a very good liar. But at least he was talking. Her grip on her gun relaxed. Whatever the situation was here, she was certain that this man posed no immediate threat to her, or that Danny Sabatini was behind them with a gun pointed at his head.

"Is this Mr. Sabatini's sister?" Claire said, motioning with her head to the woman hovering behind him.

The man's head withdrew briefly as if unsure which woman Claire was talking about. When the head returned the door was held open a little wider and Claire could not only see the woman who had originally opened the door, but also the reception room behind them. Empty.

"Yes I am," the woman said. "I… I'm Danny's sister."

Claire tried to work out just what the situation was.

Just then, Wilson rejoined her, both sets of eyes going to her partner, the sight of the tall, dark-haired agent making them even more nervous. A small whine escaped from the woman's taut mouth.

Wilson gave a very slight shake of his head, indicating there was nothing to report from the rear of the house.

"This is Mr. Sabatini's sister and brother-in-law. They inform me that Danny is inside the house, but is too ill to see anybody," Claire said, addressing her partner.

"Is that right, agent?" Wilson said.

"Doctor's orders," the man said, his wife nodding vehemently in agreement behind him.

"Let me have the name of the doctor. I will speak to him myself," Claire said.

The husband and wife seemed to shrink slightly, then they looked at each other.

Claire waited, but neither said anything.

She sighed. "Look, I don't know what the situation is here, but you are clearly hiding something. You can tell me exactly what it is you are hiding or we will arrest you both, take you to the precinct, and find it out that way. Either way, believe me, we will get to the bottom of whatever charade you two are trying to pull here."

"Danny is too ill to see anybody…" the man repeated, but even he had lost faith in his words, and they tailed off.

Claire decided to go for a change of approach. "We are investigating multiple homicides. We have evidence to believe Danny Sabatini, your brother-in-law and a man registered as living at this abode, can help us with getting to the bottom of the investigation."

Her words had an effect, but not the one she had expected.

"Homicide?" the husband and wife echoed as one, nerves and fear replaced by confusion.

"Danny can't help you…" the man said, looking at his wife and nodding slightly.

"Why not? I am losing patience fast," Claire said.

"Because he is dead," the woman said. "Danny is dead."

Claire looked at her.

It was the first words that had come out of the mouths of the couple that Claire believed. But how could that be? Had he taken his own life, guilt at his actions catching up with him? Had his sister and brother-in-law discovered his terrible secret and done it themselves? Neither of those seemed plausible.

The pair sagged in front of her, their faces seeming to age in a matter of seconds. The man opened the door wide, stepping back to allow Claire to step in.

"You had better come in," he said.

Claire and Wilson followed the couple through to a large modern kitchen, positioning themselves opposite the couple across from an island that sat in the middle of the floor, a sink in the middle of it.

The husband and wife looked at each other. Tears were in the woman's eyes, while the man looked like he was going to be sick.

Claire watched as he sucked in a deep breath, his hands steadying himself on the work surface in front of him.

"Ok," he said. "Time to come clean I guess." He looked to his wife next to him, who nodded, noticing a tear that rolled down her face. He put his hand on top of hers, before addressing Claire again.

"Danny died three years ago. He was sick. Had been sick for years. All his life. Lead in his system. From the water he drank every day when he was just a young boy. He knew he would never get better."

“Three years ago?” Claire said. Then it dawned on her. The nervousness, the wealthy area.

The man’s next words confirmed it.

“We have… we have been cashing his disability checks. We… we never registered the death. My cousin runs a crematorium. We burnt the body. We…”

“My brother was killed by the city, by the people who refused to give him clean drinking water; that isn’t too much to ask is it? In this day and age?” the woman, Danny’s sister said, anger giving her voice a strength they hadn’t heard before. “We were only taking back what we were owed,” she said looking at the two agents defiantly.

“And spending it on this lifestyle?” Claire said. “What happened to your brother was wrong, but don’t hide behind that to defend your actions. What you have done, and would have continued to do if we hadn’t come along this morning, has nothing to do with your brother’s suffering, and everything to do with your greed.” Claire turned away in disgust, angry more at the time wasted on this dead end, frustrated more at another door closing on the case than the actions of this foolish, greedy couple.

“Come on, agent,” Claire said, leading the way out of the kitchen. “You can expect a call from our uniformed colleagues shortly,” she called over her shoulder at the husband and wife who were in each other’s arms, hugging.

Claire quickened her pace as they strode down the drive to their car.

“There is a murderer out there,” she said, gesturing with her hand at the city at large. “What are we going to do now to catch him?”

CHAPTER EIGHTEEN

A man, dressed in a Colorado Rockies sweatshirt, crossed the pedestrian walkway in front of him. The rumble of loud music, filtered through cheap car speakers, steel, and glass made the Rockies fan look to his left. Right into his eyes.

The look on the man's face, the sheer shock at what he saw made him veer away. He took one more quick look to make sure his eyes hadn't played a trick on him, then broke into a run, escaping to the safety of the sidewalk, the safety of fellow pedestrians.

In the driver's seat, he watched the pathetic creature cower from the sight of him. Cringe at the power he exuded, caged in this rust bucket of a car.

The thought sent a fleeting feeling of pride washing over his jangling nerves and twitching body, but it was almost instantly swept aside by the black rage that had complete control of every part of him now.

He snarled at the retreating figure's back, his head twisting on his neck looking for others that he could latch his anger onto.

A young couple, hand in hand, came out of a designer clothing store. They were laughing, sharing a joke as they strolled down the sidewalk, not a care in the world.

He gripped the handle of the door, ready to leap out onto the sidewalk, to give them a whole lot of things they would care about, that they would care and cry about for the rest of their privileged and pathetic lives.

Then the red light changed to green, and he remembered what he was doing. Where he was going.

There would be time to teach them a lesson later. The only thing that mattered now was where he was going. What he was going to do. And who he was going to do it to.

He beat his fists into his thighs, enjoying the pain it gave him, using the pressure released via the valves of his fists to gain control. He gave one final look at the couple then slammed his foot down on the gas, shrieking along with the song blasting out of the stereo as it hit the chorus.

Dust on the filthy dashboard jumped in time with the heavy drumbeat; stringent guitars echoed around the small interior.

His body was in tune with the music. The aggression and pure power of the wave of noise plugged into his nervous system, so that his emotions rose and fell with the sounds. In between songs he would suddenly feel cast adrift, a young baby reaching for the comforting embrace of his mother, before being swept along with the next crushing guitar riff.

He had always been drawn to the intensity of rock music, the way it could elevate his emotions to dangerous heights. It was a primal force, one that spoke directly to him, gave him a release that he craved more than anything else in this world. And today, he needed it more than ever before.

As the song reached its climax, he felt a surge of adrenaline coursing through his veins. His hand fumbled with the stereo controls, trying to twist the volume button higher, but it was already as loud as it would go.

Thwarted by the stupid piece of plastic, he wrenched it off, throwing it at the windshield, the round plastic button bouncing off and into the seat beside him.

His eyes followed it. They rested on the two bottles. One with chloroform, one with something that would send his next victim to sleep forever. Beside them lay a heavy chain, and beside that, a pair of handcuffs.

The sight of these tools, instruments in his plan, usually calmed his anger, reduced the ball of red hot magma in his gut, but this time they only reminded him of the injustices, of the power imbalances that had defined his life.

Throwing his head back he screamed at the roof just inches above him. His hand thrashing at the door beside him, the fingers on his other hand, the one gripping the steering wheel white as he gripped harder and harder.

He wrenched the wheel one way then the other, the car swerving recklessly in and out of the traffic. He screamed at anyone who dared to look at him, driving the heel of his hand into his forehead again and again, vaguely in time with the music, but mostly in response to the anger he could feel trying to crack open his skull.

Through all of this angry, swirling, tumultuous fog, one crystal clear thought shone through: he address where the next person who would be taught a lesson lived.

Somewhere deep inside him, beneath the insanity that drove all of his other motions and emotions, there was a part that latched onto that address and was steering the car, guiding its master to it. Taking the correct route, avoiding stationary vehicles, swerving past moving ones.

Managing to keep a grip on his mind and his limbs stopped him from slamming on the brakes, jumping out of his battered car, and unleashing his rage on the nearest people he could find.

It was that one remaining part of him, the last part to be completely frazzled and eaten up by the anger, that would ensure he was able to carry out the next part of his plan.

The building that corresponded to that very same address was visible on the right.

A rictus of a smile stretched across his face, and he yanked the wheel, a screech of tires accompanying him as he entered the parking lot.

CHAPTER NINETEEN

"Stop the car, Wilson!" Claire urged, her hand gripping his arm to back up the words.

Wilson's eyes flew to his mirrors and his head swiveled around on his neck, trying to see what it was that his partner had seen.

"What? What is it?" he said, his foot stepping on the brake and pulling into the side of a gas station.

Claire released her grip on Wilson's arm and pulled her fingers through her hair.

"I've been thinking," she said, trying to choose her words carefully. "The vision I had. The number 212…"

"The one that led us to the basement where Jennifer Mannings was?" Wilson said, turning to face her.

"Well yes…" Claire said, pursing her lips. "But I'm starting to think that was a coincidence. Or maybe that was why the numbers were so random; maybe they were pointing to two different places?" She blew out her breath in frustration, as usual not comfortable discussing something so ephemeral as the visions.

She watched a father and son walk along the sidewalk. The boy, in his early teens she guessed, was bouncing a basketball as he made his way alongside his dad. In the midst of all the crazy, upsetting and downright horrific incidents that were happening in the city, that innocent, tiny snatch of normality made her heart soar.

"Up until now, the visions, in this case anyway, have been centered around the killer. I'm still convinced that boy in the hospital is our man, despite our search of the hospital records not turning anyone up apart from Sabatini," she said, tearing her eyes off the family and looking at Wilson.

He gave a slow nod. "We both knew the records weren't complete. I guess we were just hoping it wouldn't matter, as we had our man anyway."

It was Claire's turn to nod in agreement.

As they sat in the car, the silence between them grew heavy with the weight of their failure. Despite what they thought had looked like progress, all three murders were still unsolved, and they were back to square one. Claire's mind raced with the possibilities; maybe the numbers were referencing another victim, or the killer's next attempt. She shuddered at the thought of another innocent life being taken by their elusive suspect.

Then her mind went back to the thread she had been trying to work out. If that vision *was* linked to the killer, and nothing to do with Jennifer Mannings, what did that mean?

Her gaze settled on Wilson, and she saw he was staring intently at her, waiting for her to expand on what she had said. She suddenly realized how much expectation was on her to come up with the solution, the answer to their dilemma of who was carrying out these brutal killings. It was extra pressure she certainly didn't need, but she could do nothing about it.

"What if the number was pointing to that building for another reason? Was that the building where the killer had lived? Where he had suffered whatever trauma had cracked his mind, and was the motivation for him to do what he did to Daniel Walsh, Tommy Jacobson, and Jennifer Mannings, and undoubtedly will do to others if he isn't caught?" She took a breath, trying to make sense of the thoughts whirling in her head.

"What if," she continued, her hand going to the crook of Wilson's arm, "there is another block 212, or even if it's the same one, the fact Jennifer Mannings was killed in it is just coincidence… or further proof even that the building is where it all began… look, I know I'm not making much sense…" she trailed off.

"No, no, I get what you're saying," Wilson said. "If that building is the key, or another tenement block that is number 212 is the key, then we just need to go through the records of residents, see if any run up a red flag."

Claire's mind shot back to the building they had found Jennifer Mannings in. It was one of the older blocks in the city, certainly old enough to have been the home to the boy in the hospital twenty-five or so years ago.

The two agents looked at each other, he frustration of just a couple of minutes ago erased with this new plan of attack.

Wilson shoved the car into drive and shot back out into the traffic.

***

"That block, 212 Aurora Drive, is the only one it could be," Wilson said walking around the desk to Claire.

"If our theory is right..." she said, taking her eyes off the lists of residents on her laptop screen.

"At the minute all we can do is to assume we *are* right..." he said, not needing to spell out the consequences if they weren't. "The only other block that has number 212 in the whole of the greater Denver area was built just six years ago. Before that it was a brake pad factory. If the killer lived at 212, it's someone on that list," he said pointing to Claire's screen and crouching down beside his partner.

Claire felt her mood lift. Not only because the task had just become easier, but also because of the enthusiasm of Wilson. The incident in the hotel bar came back briefly, but she shoved it aside, her mind once again focusing purely on the list in front of her.

"I've taken a ten-year period," she said. "If that doesn't give us anything, we can go back further." Her fingers flew over the keys, the screen split between two lists.

"Just give me... a... couple... of... minutes..." she said, sucking in her top lip, her eyes darting from one list to the other, the cursor highlighting one name, dragging it across, dropping it, going back to the list again.

"I'm going through the tenants, matching them with those who have been confirmed with lead poisoning...Seeing if coming at it from the other angle will throw any light. There are so many anomalies in these records, so many holes, I get the feeling every different direction we come at it will give us something new." She pointed to three names written on her pad.

Wilson watched, entranced as the cursor moved with blurring speed, trying to follow his partner as she flicked from name to name, discounting each one.

Three minutes later, she pushed back from the desk.

"Three names," she said. "Let's see what these give us."

She brought up a new window on her laptop. Typed in the first name.

Both sets of eyes devoured the information that popped up on the screen. Both hearts dropped when they saw that he was in the Army, in active service, based in South Korea.

The next two names seemed to be related. Father and son, or possibly brothers.

The first name produced another wave of disappointment. Steven Fleck had died twenty-two years ago.

Claire's eyes went to the third name on the list. Robert Fleck.

His details came up on the screen. Both agents held their breath, as they skimmed the details.

"He's still alive..." Claire muttered, "lives locally..."

"He is the brother of Steven. He died...that fits in..." Wilson said.

Claire nodded, determined not to let her mind run away, to jump to conclusions, to grasp at something because she was desperate, not because that was where the evidence pointed.

She brought up more records on Robert Fleck.

"That was why he didn't come up on our initial searches," she said pointing to the screen. "His diagnosis was never disclosed. The place he was treated was more of a clinic by the looks of it. His family was too poor to afford actual health care..."

"It shut down twenty years ago," Wilson pointed out.

"And they don't appear to have kept any records..." Claire said shaking her head.

She brought up a picture of Robert Fleck on her screen, stared at it, trying to marry it up with the man she saw in her vision raging against the world.

The face in the vision was too indistinct. But there was something about the man that stared out of the screen at her that made her think they were staring at the man who had chained those three landlords to radiators and subjected each of them to a terrible death.

CHAPTER TWENTY

With the blue light on the roof and the heel of Wilson's hand slamming on the horn, the car made light work of the midday traffic, as it sliced its way towards Robert Fleck's registered address. Claire gripped the armrest as the car roared through downtown, the neighborhood changing to one that featured the all too familiar groups of men on the corners.

The tension in the streets would again be taut, but at that moment Claire did not care, nor she imagined, did Wilson.

There was nothing worse in a case than not doing anything. Sitting there, waiting for events, or more often than not, the killer to make the move which would determine *your* next one. Reacting as opposed to acting. Now they were doing something. Positive.

Claire felt frustration at not realizing the true implication of the vision with the numbers before. Wilson had told her that there was absolutely nothing for her to beat herself up about. He'd said she couldn't have known that was what the images were pointing at, that this was still completely new territory; it was like learning a whole new language. But Claire wasn't made like that. She had been given all the pieces of the puzzle, and had failed to put them together in the way that would show them who the killer was.

Because of that, Jennifer Mannings had lost her life.

That was something that Claire would have to carry around with her for the rest of *her* life.

Now though, they had found the name of the man responsible. She had something to go on. She was doing something to bring justice to bear.

As they pulled up to the address, Claire's heart was pounding in her chest. She could almost taste the adrenaline coursing through her body. The house, less than two miles from where Jonny Cairns lived, was a dilapidated two-story building with peeling paint. One of its windows was boarded up, and Claire's first thought was that the property was abandoned, that it was Fleck's home in name only.

But then, as she stepped out of the car, she could see there were signs of recent life in the front yard.

She gripped the handle of her gun, her eyes scanning the area for any signs of movement.

"Are you ready for this?" Wilson asked, his eyes fixed on the house.

Claire gave a terse nod in reply, then, gun drawn, approached the door of the house.

The doorbell delivered a flat ring, a noise that was accompanied by the hammering of Claire's fist on the filthy paintwork.

There was no sound. Wilson motioned that he was going around the back when the door to the house on the right opened and a harassed looking woman with two young children at her heels walked out into her front yard.

Claire returned her attention to the house in front of her, eyes scanning for signs of movement.

"He ain't in."

Claire looked to the woman who had shouted across.

"Sorry ma'am, what did you say?" she called, her gun pointing to the ground, hidden by her body, but still poised for action should anything – or anyone – suddenly burst from the house. Beside her Wilson stopped, but like Claire he was still giving more than half his attention to the property listed as Robert Fleck's.

"He ain't in," the woman repeated, pulling one of her children up by the arm as he tried to sit on the ground. "Saw him leave twenty minutes ago. Driving that old wreck of his. That music blastin' out as usual, enough to wake the dead." She seemed to suddenly notice that both Fleck's visitors were carrying guns, but more unusually, Claire guessed, both were smartly dressed.

"What you want with him? Knew he was bad news the moment I laid eyes on 'im," she said.

"Stay there," Claire said in a low tone to Wilson, before walking over to the woman. Both the children looked up at her, as she holstered her gun, the firearm replaced in her hand by her cell phone. She brought up a picture of Fleck on its screen and held it up for the woman to look at.

"Is that the man who lives there?" Claire asked, indicating the house behind her.

The woman's face screwed up as she peered at the screen, her hand shielding it from the glare of the sun which was almost directly overhead.

Then she gave a firm nod of her head. "That's 'im alright," she said, then peered at Claire with the same intensity she had at the cell phone screen. "What you want 'im for?"

“We hope he can help us with an investigation we are working on. Does he live alone?”

“You bet he does. Who’s gunna wanna live with trash like ‘im?”

“Ok, thanks for your help, ma’am,” Claire said, returning to Wilson. Behind her the woman looked like she was ready to settle down and enjoy whatever show the two agents were going to put on.

“It’s his place alright,” Claire said, then punched in the number for the police chief.

“This is Agent Claire King,” she said when the chief picked up on the second ring. “We are at the suspect’s house for the homicide of Daniel Walsh, Tommy Jacobson, and Jennifer Mannings. The suspect is a Robert Fleck,” Claire said before giving the address and those details she had for him. “The suspect left his home approximately twenty minutes ago. I need you to put out an APB for his vehicle. Note that it may also have loud music playing.”

She walked around to the side of the house, eyes searching for a way in. “Agent Wilson and I are going to enter the property.” She ended the call, as Wilson joined her.

At the rear of the house there was a door, which like the front one was covered in dirty, white, peeling paint. Claire tried the handle, but it was locked. She caught Wilson’s eye, knew he was thinking the same thing. If there was anything inside that could lead them to where Fleck had gone, it was worth crossing any lines. They could deal with the fallout afterwards. The only thing that mattered at that moment was that the number of victims remain at three.

Claire wrapped the handle of her gun in her jacket and smashed the filthy window, then used it to clear the shards that remained in the frame. She then reached through and opened it.

She entered the dirty, stale smelling kitchen, gun pointing out in front of her. She waited a couple of thudding heartbeats to allow her eyes to adjust to the gloom.

The kitchen was filthy, but it had certainly been used in the last few hours. The dripping tap in the sink had only half filled a pan, a scum of grease resting on the discolored water. She stepped stealthily and quietly further inside, Wilson two steps behind her. The neighbor had said the house was empty, but she only had her word for it. He may have come back, unnoticed by the harassed mother of two. He may have someone else in the house.

Either way, they were dealing with a serial killer and couldn’t take any chances.

The kitchen opened up into a square hallway. A bathroom, smaller and more squalid than the kitchen, was to the immediate right, the open door showing it was empty. A flight of stairs led off to the left, with two more rooms downstairs.

Claire motioned for Wilson to take those, while she stepped onto the first stair, testing the thin carpeted wood with her weight. It creaked as she slowly and as quietly as she could, made her way upstairs, her gun pointing the way.

The stairs twisted back on themselves, revealing a landing above.

Empty.

At the top of the stairs she was faced with three doorways. Two open, one closed. The nearest one was to a bathroom, bigger than the one downstairs, but one that was no more familiar with the scent of bleach. Her eyes flicked off the stained walls, staying there long enough to ascertain it was empty and not a second more.

The next room looked like it was the room Fleck used as a bedroom. It had a mattress on the floor, the filthy carpet hidden under piles of worn cloths, and ripped up pages from magazines and newspapers. Two large dents in the wall and one in the door told their own story.

That left one more room.

She could hear Wilson downstairs opening a door, as she went up to the closed one on her floor. The handle was cool to her touch, but opened with no resistance. She flung the door open, sweeping her gun to the left and right.

The room was empty. Completely empty. There was no furniture and it was the only room she had seen in the house that wasn't filthy or where the floor was littered with trash.

The drapes were closed, only a thin beam of light forcing its way through the cheap material. She walked over to them and yanked the one on her right, the rusty curtain rings catching and stalling the action. It had been enough to open them a few inches though and the light flooded in, picking up the dust motes that hung thickly in the stale air.

Claire took in what the light revealed, her eyes searching for something, anything, that would give a clue, an insight into the man who called this home.

She turned, faced the wall opposite the window, and stopped.

"Wilson!" she shouted. "Up here!"

She could hear Wilson's heavy footsteps racing up the stairs as she took in the sight in front of her, then her partner burst in through the door, his own gun drawn.

Claire pointed to the wall with her eyes.

The beige paintwork was all but obscured by photographs, newspaper cuttings, and magazine articles. They were stuck in a seemingly haphazard fashion, some had been obliterated with the thick red ink from a sharpie.

The sources of the material may have been varied, but there was a common theme.

Or rather, two common themes. In between articles, some dating back years, even decades, on lead poisoning and various scandals that had rocked public housing projects in the city over the years, were blown up photographs of individuals. Three of them were instantly recognizable to Claire. She had seen two stretched out on gurneys at the coroner's. The other, that of Jennifer Mannings, she had seen chained to a radiator in a basement of the tenement block that Robert Fleck had grown up in.

The block whose water system had killed his brother, and nearly killed him.

But they weren't the pictures that Claire ran over to. There were two photographs of people Claire did not recognize. A woman in her thirties, and a man who looked to be in his sixties at least. Beside them were their names and addresses.

Claire knew that she was looking at the fourth and fifth victims of Robert Fleck. Or they would be unless she could prevent it.

She got on her cell phone immediately, reading out the details of both intended victims, hoping with all her being that they could be contacted and moved to a safe space until the killer was caught.

"Hold please," the voice on the line said. Claire knew that the two people whose faces stared down from the wall in front of her were being traced as she stood there, that the right calls were being made, but it did not make it any less frustrating. She felt useless standing there, listening to the silence on the phone. Impotent.

The silence stretched out to the point where she was convinced the call had been cut off, when the voice came back.

"Agent King?" the woman's annoyingly calm voice said.

"Yes I'm here, have you traced those two people?" she asked, her voice urgent, her hand tight around the phone.

"We have spoken to Sally Ryder. She is at her sister's and an officer is on his way there now." There was a pause and Claire felt her tension rising even more. "We have not been able to trace the second individual, Clint Goldmann. Officers have been dispatched to his home address."

Claire closed her eyes, the words hanging ominously in the air. She thanked the woman, demanded to be kept informed, then relayed the news to Wilson who was studying the pictures on the wall.

She walked over to them, her eyes skimming the text, both that which was written in a journalist's office, and angrily scrawled by the owner of this house. Some had been ripped, others torn off the wall completely in the frenzied scribblings. Some of the additions weren't even words, just faces or names obliterated, other sections of text underlined or circled.

At her feet were the sheets and articles that had been ripped off.

She stooped to pick one up, one that looked like it was from the local newspaper, its yellowing pages indicating its age.

As Claire's fingers grasped the dry paper, the breath was sucked out of her as the room fell away, slipping from her consciousness. She was suddenly in the midst of an awful scene. Seemingly inches away from her was the killer. His face was distorted with rage, but she could now clearly see it was the same face that had stared out at her from her laptop screen less than an hour ago. Robert Fleck.

He was screaming at someone hunched down on the floor next to him. Claire couldn't see the face of the man, but from the way he was sitting, from his clothes and the mottled skin on his hands, she could tell it was an old man.

"DRINK IT! DRINK IT!" he bawled, his whole face, neck and body rigid, tensed like a steel cable.

Then, thankfully, the awful scene vanished and she was back in the bedroom. She was still crouched on the floor, but her legs felt like jelly, and she lowered herself to the floor, her back resting against the cool wall, her head on her knees.

"Claire! Claire? Are you ok?" Wilson was crouching beside her, his hand gently touching her forehead. It felt hot.

She sucked some air into her lungs, not sure which part of her needed it most, her weak body or whirling mind.

"What did you see?" Wilson's voice was soft, soothing even, despite the nature and urgency of the question.

She looked at him, feeling sweat suddenly leaping from the pores of her skin on her forehead, on her upper lip.

"He's got him. He's got Goldmann," she said, summoning every inch of power to push herself up from the floor.

Suddenly the cell phone which sat forgotten, clasped in her clammy hand, buzzed, almost making her spill it to the ground.

"Have you reached Mr. Goldmann?" she almost shouted into the phone.

"… is this Agent King?" a confused male voice said on the other line.

"Yes, this is Agent King, go ahead," Claire said, lowering her voice, wishing she could do the same to her racing heartbeat.

"We have a hit on your APB. We have located Robert Fleck's vehicle."

CHAPTER TWENTY ONE

The dam that had been on the brink of bursting the entire time they had been in the city had finally ruptured. Whether by a coordinated message, or simply as a result of the tension having to go somewhere, large parts of the city had erupted in a new level of unrest and violence.

Whole neighborhoods had been taken over by gangs of youth and angry men and women. Fueled by fury, feelings of injustice, and the frustrations of a bleak future stretching out in front of them, they now had the added confidence that the streets were theirs. It wasn't that there was lawlessness in the city. They *were* the law. And Claire and Wilson knew that was a volatile and dangerous mix.

Opting not to use the lights or siren, not wanting to draw any attention to themselves, Wilson threw the car around the streets that were either eerily deserted or dangerously full. It was a surreal feeling, but Claire knew that this was only the backdrop to what their mission was. To save Clint Goldmann and to take down Robert Fleck, dead or alive.

The nightmarish scenes that flashed by the windows, the screaming sirens that seemed to be coming from everywhere, and the screeching tires of their own vehicle were joined in Claire's head by the sounds and images from her awful vision.

Wilson took the ninety-degree turn at fifty miles an hour, and for a second Claire was convinced the car would either roll or slam into the boarded up liquor store that loomed closer and closer to her window and door.

Gripping the wheel with white-knuckled fingers, his body thrown halfway onto Claire's seat, he just managed to keep the vehicle under control. It had barely straightened up when he slammed his foot back down on the gas and they were thrown back in their seats once again.

Two minutes later he slammed on his brakes. The road ahead was blocked, a burning car blocking one side of the highway, a group of twenty, thirty men blocking the rest. They were armed with everything and anything they could get hold of, and Claire could see those that weren't turned towards them being nudged and spun around. Even from twenty yards away, she could feel the violence and intent on their faces, in the body language.

Bricks and metal poles rained down on the road in front of them.

Wilson shoved the car into reverse, turning in his seat as they hurtled backwards, hoping against hope that another group hadn't come in behind them and closed off their escape route.

Claire watched as several of the men in front broke into a run and she could hear Wilson beside her mutter "come on, come on," his voice tense.

"Hold on," he said, and swung the car around, heading perpendicular to the road they'd just come back out of.

They were heading in the right direction again, but had lost valuable minutes. Claire was suddenly struck by another thought.

"There's no way any officers are gonna attend the APB. Every man and woman is going to be dealing with this," she said, pointing to the city outside the windows.

"I was thinking exactly the same thing," Wilson said, hitting the brakes and skidding around a corner.

They both let out relieved sighs as the road ahead was clear. The caller had informed Claire that Fleck's vehicle had been located in the parking lot of a tenement block, two blocks from where Tommy Jacobson had been killed; but what should have been a fifteen minute journey had already taken more than twenty.

Three minutes later, Wilson screeched to a halt next to Fleck's car. Their fears had been correct. There was no sign of any police cruiser. Mercifully this block was quiet, but whoever had called the APB in had been ordered away.

They were on their own, but that was neither nothing new nor something that they could let distract them.

The building loomed up above them, and when they ran into the small, rank smelling lobby, it was deserted.

Claire raced down the dark stairwell, Wilson thudding behind her. The light was broken or had been disabled, and they hadn't had time to get a flashlight or even use the ones on their cell phones.

She skidded to a stop in front of the door which she knew led to the basement. It was the type of door she had become all too familiar with since her arrival in the Mile High City.

The silence that filled the vacuum left by their running feet was suddenly filled with something far more alarming. Through the metal door, somewhere at the far end of the basement, both agents could hear the terrible scene being played out.

The distorted commands by the man they knew was Robert Fleck, and the animal grunts and cries from the one they knew was Clint Goldmann.

The vision that Claire had back in Fleck's house allowed her mind to fill in the visual pieces. It was not something she welcomed.

"He's alive," Claire said, out of breath from both the sprint and the high altitude. "He's still alive."

Wilson twisted the door handle, pulling and pushing the steel door, but unable to budge it. Claire groped for her cell phone, shining the light from it at the door that sat stubbornly closed in front of them.

The sounds from the other side continued. She could hear Fleck imploring his next victim to drink the poisonous cocktail he had prepared for him.

She saw Wilson draw his gun, but she put her hand on his, shaking her head.

"He will have barricaded it. Same as the windows." In her mind's eye she could see the planks of wood, screwed into the door frame.

Claire's heart pounded in her chest as she thought of a way to get into the basement. She scanned the dark stairwell, her eyes landing on the fire extinguisher that was mounted on the wall. She quickly grabbed it, motioning for Wilson to stand back.

With one swift motion, she slammed the fire extinguisher into the door handle. Then at the four corners of the door. After several blows, Wilson suddenly came to life, the heels of his boots then his shoulders adding to the clamor of metallic bangs and dull thuds that echoed around the cramped gloomy stairwell.

The metal groaned in protest, then this was added to by the dry crack of splintering wood, and then a final swing of the extinguisher as the door swung open.

Gun in one hand, cell phone in the other casting a slender beam of light, Claire rushed into the dark, cavernous basement.

"FBI!" she shouted into the dank space. "Drop your weapon."

A thin splinter of sunshine shone in from a crack in a large piece of wood over a window straight ahead, illuminating the basement slightly, though it was still a room of shadows, of dark corners.

Claire turned off her cell phone light, not wanting to present a target. She had no idea if Fleck was armed but had to assume he was.

Her eyes found the radiator, the familiar shape of the large cast iron fins. It was fixed to the wall, just to the right of the window.

But Clint Goldmann was not chained to it.

Then, movement and a groan to her right made her swing her attention and her gun to its source.

The first thing she saw was a pair of eyes. Huge white eyes, extended in pure terror. They were looking right at Claire, but she was not sure they were seeing her. The expression on the man's face, on Glen Goldmann's face, didn't change.

It was the expression of a man who had seen death. Had seen it and knew it didn't always come peacefully.

Quickly, Claire's mind filled in the rest of the details. Goldmann sat on the floor, his legs stretched out in front of him. Around his neck was an arm, the hand at the end of the arm held a long knife, its serrated blade pushed into the exposed throat of the elderly gentleman. Claire could see his Adam's apple, bobbing up and down as he swallowed desperately.

Across the man's chest was another arm; the hand on the end of that one held a metal flask. Claire didn't need to see the contents of the flask to know it was filled with lead shavings.

Behind the head of Goldmann was that of Robert Fleck.

The manic rage that had consumed Fleck appeared to have given way to a steely resolve. When Claire met his eyes, it wasn't madness she saw in there but determination. A single-minded fortitude to finish what he had begun, no matter what or who tried to get in his way.

The knife still against the thin tissue of Goldmann's neck, Fleck angled the open flask, bringing it up to the old man's quivering lips.

"Drink it," he hissed. "Drink it. It's a little concoction I've made just for you. Just for you and your murderous cohorts. It's called revenge. Drink it. DRINK IT!" The last words were screamed into the ear of Goldmann, just two inches from the mouth that barked the command. They were evidence, if she needed it, that his madness, that uncontrollable frenzied rage, was not far away. Was always bubbling below the surface.

"Put the knife down Fleck," Claire said, her voice steady, the gun equally steady, pointed between the eyes of Fleck. She inched forward, slowly, gradually covering the distance between her and the two men on the floor, five yards away.

Wilson stood beside her, his gun also held out in front. There was enough distance between the two agents to force Fleck to have to flick his eyes between them. It was exactly what they wanted. As they inched closer, they also increased the gap between themselves.

"Put the knife down. Put the flask down. It's over," Claire said, her voice commanding but non-aggressive. Textbook.

“Put the flask down, Robert,” Wilson said, taking up the narrative, causing Fleck’s head to swivel towards the FBI agent. “Even if you make him drink it, we will have medics here in no time. They’ll pump his stomach. He will be fine.”

“I’ve got this!” Fleck growled, pushing the knife’s blade further into Goldmann’s neck, causing him to swallow, the Adam’s apple bobbing up and down again.

“That isn’t the way you planned it though, is it?” Claire said. The head swiveled back to her and, out of the corner of her eye, she could see Wilson taking advantage by taking a half-step forward.

“Stabbing Mr. Goldmann is not going to get revenge for what happened to your brother. For what happened to you. That’s not what all this is about is it? Where’s the resolution in that?” Claire said, her voice gentle now.

Confusion, incomprehension washed over Fleck’s face. She could see him trying to work out whether or not what she said was true.

She took a half-step forward. Her foot kicked something on the concrete ground, sending it skidding towards the two men on the floor. All four pairs of eyes peered through the gloom at what it was.

Claire realized it was the top of the flask, the flask still held to Goldmann’s lips.

It seemed to bring Fleck to his senses slightly, suddenly aware of the situation.

“Stop where you are, or I swear I’ll kill him!” he shouted, his eyes darting back and forth between Claire and Wilson.

Claire stopped in her tracks, holding her breath as she tried to think of a way to diffuse the situation. She could feel her heart pounding in her chest as she watched Fleck's eyes flicker with a dangerous intensity. In that moment, she knew that one wrong move could lead to Goldmann's death.

“Robert, put down the knife," Wilson said, his voice low and steady. "We can help you. We can get you the justice you deserve, but you have to let Mr. Goldmann go."

Fleck's eyes narrowed as he glanced between the two FBI agents. His grip on the flask tightened.

Claire took a deep breath and spoke calmly, "Robert, I know you're hurting. I know you want revenge for what happened to your brother. But this isn't the way. Killing an innocent man won't bring your brother back. It won't bring you peace."

“He is not innocent,” Fleck hissed. “Lining their pockets while they are lining children’s bodies with lead.”

He stared wildly at Claire, at Wilson, then back to Claire, daring them to contradict him.

Then he hauled Clint Goldmann up, bringing his own legs underneath him, the old man being held, his legs dangling beneath him like a doll.

"Drop your guns, or he gets it. I don't care what happens to me anymore, but one false move and he won't draw another stinking breath."

Claire could see that he meant it and lowered her gun, but still held onto it. She could see Wilson doing the same.

Goldmann let out a whimper as he tried to get his feet onto the floor, to take some of the weight, away from the knife held at his throat.

Then two things happened almost simultaneously. Both accompanied by a roar that came from the very depths of Robert Fleck's soul.

He flung the contents of the flask at Claire, the warm liquid covering her face, neck, and chest. She recoiled, her mind grasping at the possibility, slim though it was, that the flask contained acid, not lead shavings suspended in water. The tiny metal fragments covered her face like a mask, forcing her to breathe in the metallic tang they carried with them. She clawed at her eyes, dredging the fragments out, blinking furiously, at the same time coughing and spitting as her body spontaneously reacted.

A split second after flinging the flask at Claire, Fleck shoved Clint Goldmann at Wilson. The old man's body struck the agent, catching him off guard and sending the two of them spinning to the ground. Goldmann landed on top of the agent, his face smacking into the floor next to Wilson, his face and nose making a terrible sound as it connected with the concrete floor.

Claire was aware of movement to her right as she regained her senses and sight. She saw Wilson on the ground, Goldmann spread on top of him, bleeding from his nose and seemingly unconscious.

She spun around, to see Fleck sprinting towards the door, hurdling the splintered wood he had screwed across it half an hour earlier, and disappearing into the pitch black maw of the stairwell.

"Make sure Goldmann's OK," she cried, setting off towards the doorway herself. "I'll get Fleck."

CHAPTER TWENTY TWO

Claire emerged at the top of the stairwell, suddenly blinded by the sunlight, her gun out in front, her body tensed for the kick to the wrist. A punch to the stomach. Or worse, the cold steel of the knife.

But the foyer was empty.

Three strides took her outside, her eyes desperately searching the sidewalks left, right, and in front for the fleeing figure of Robert Fleck.

He was nowhere.

Her hand grabbed for her cell phone to call for backup, even though she knew it was unlikely, but it came up empty, and she realized she must have dropped it when Fleck had thrown the flask's contents at her. The parking lot was to the left of the building and she raced there, quickly identifying Fleck's car, still there. The lot was otherwise deserted. No hiding places. He wasn't there. There was no sign of him on any of the sidewalks in that direction. He must have gone the other way.

She could hear sirens in the distance, but still this block at least was free of the roving gangs that had taken over much of this part of the city.

She raced back, knowing every second was vital. He had already had a five, perhaps ten-second head start. She had wasted another ten seconds searching for him in the parking lot. She took off for the other side of the building, head craning to the left and right, eyes scanning every possible place for the killer.

The area to the immediate right of the tenement block was a wasteland. A sign, sporting the DPG logo, promised an exciting new residential project. Next to that was another block, one that looked to be in the process of demolition. A process that had been halted either due to financial circumstances or the social climate on the streets of the city.

Then, just as she was giving up hope of finding him, she spotted the red hoodie of Fleck. He was in the deserted lot, sprinting towards the safety of the other side, which Claire knew contained a labyrinth of alleyways and side streets. If he made it to that, she would never find him.

She raised her gun, took aim at the fleeing figure sixty yards away, and pulled the trigger.

There was a puff of dust in a pile of rubble just to the right of her target, as the shot rang out, echoing off the buildings. Fleck threw himself to the floor, looking back towards where the shot had come from. She watched him get to his knees, then head in a stooping sprint towards the cover of the dilapidated building to his right.

Claire aimed again, but the crouching, swerving figure offered a tiny, moving target. She set off after him instead, heading for the knocked-out side entrance that she guessed Fleck was also heading for.

Her feet flew over the rubble and garbage-strewn uneven ground, hurdling a rusted metal pole that jutted out from a concrete block. She had cut Fleck's head start. He was heading to the doorway – which was no more than a hole punched into the side of the building – at right angles, while she was sprinting towards it at a forty five degree angle.

She also had the benefit of being able to run, whereas, the hunted prey was forced to run in a cowering posture so as to reduce the size of target he presented.

She watched as he finally straightened up, taking a last look behind him, and he disappeared through the hole in the wall.

She was now only fifteen yards behind.

Claire slowed her pace as she approached the ragged hole in the wall, her senses on high alert. She could hear the sound of Fleck's footsteps echoing through the empty building, but she couldn't see him. Claire took a deep breath and stepped through the hole, gun at the ready. The air was stale and musty, and the only light came from the gaps in the crumbling walls. Once again her eyes adjusted to the dim interior. As they did, she picked out details. Crumbling staircases. Piles of rubble. An old, stained mattress.

The walls were covered with graffiti. Not the skilled artistic pieces she had seen elsewhere in the city. These were random, coarse, and aggressive threats, aimed at certain individuals, or the city or society as a whole.

Beams of light shone through gaps in the wall and ceiling. It was like stepping into another world, one abandoned by the one just a few hundred yards outside.

Her ears strained to hear the running footsteps of Fleck. But everything was silent. He must be waiting, hiding somewhere. Watching her.

She walked slowly, getting her breath, the gun held out in front, eyes scanning the walled spaces in front of her. The interior of the building had been ripped out. Some of the walls were also gone, leaving just the supporting ones. Pipework jutted out from the walls at crazy angles, like skeletal arms, groping for any intruders.

Then suddenly she heard the scraping footsteps of Fleck. He was somewhere in front of her. Behind the wall to her right. She set off, rounding the wall, scanning the gaps for the figure.

Claire raced through a doorway, leaping just in time over a hole in the floor that dropped down into a black dungeon-like basement below.

She saw him, ahead, running up a flight of stairs, taking them two at a time. She leveled her gun, but he was gone, disappearing round the corner of the stairwell, heading up another flight.

The agent sprinted after him jumping onto the third step to avoid the bottom two which had cracked badly, and bounded up, legs and arms pumping.

Three-quarters of the way up, a nauseous tiredness hit her. She knew it was the altitude, the lack of oxygen finding its way into her blood vessels. She had been expecting it, but was still not prepared for how quick it hit her. Her head spun; her legs turned to spaghetti.

With no handrails, and a sheer drop on both sides, she was close to falling, pitching sideways down onto the concrete and metal-strewn floor below. But with an immense strength of will – nothing else, willpower the only thing that saved her – she squeezed her eyes shut, forcing the dizziness out of her body, while pulling in great gulps of air, her hand going down to the cold step to give her balance.

She was also aware that every moment she delayed was another one that Robert Fleck had to make his escape. She sucked in two more deep breaths and opened her eyes. The world around her had settled, floating stars the only sign that anything was wrong.

Straightening her legs under her, she jogged up the rest of the staircase, rounding the corner onto a mezzanine that hung out precariously over the floor beneath. Fleck must have gone up another flight.

She ran upwards, taking the stairs as quickly as she dared, aware of the drops on either side, and of the steps themselves, some of which crumbled beneath her feet.

She was also all too aware that somewhere ahead of her was a serial killer.

Claire stepped out from the stairwell. This floor was the same as the ground one, with the added peril of large missing sections. She skirted one such gap, wires and what looked like air conditioning pipework spilling from the torn sections of flooring, giving her a grim reminder of post mortems she had witnessed.

Her feet crunched on the floor, adding to the sounds of the heavy breathing she was forced to do to get air into her lungs. Fleck must be on this floor, she would have heard him climb onto the level above. Several rooms – if they could be called that with half their walls, flooring, and ceilings missing – lay in front of her. She stepped forward to the nearest one, her gun held out in front of her, pointing the way.

The doorway was half obstructed by a pile of masonry, a row of plastic guttering piled up beside it. She stepped over and into the room, which was darker, making her think it was more intact than others she had seen.

The blow hit her across the shoulder and chest, her upper arm taking a lot of the force. She also saw it at the last fraction of a second, meaning she was able to turn slightly, making it more a glancing blow than a full one.

That fraction of a second was what saved her.

Even so, the force from the rebar, a reinforced steel bar used in the construction industry, sent her flying into the wall, knocked the breath out of her, and sent her gun skidding back along the corridor she had just walked along.

She locked eyes with Fleck who stood there two feet away, holding the bar, lifting it up, wielding it above his head for another blow, one that would this time split her skull.

She saw the dull metal bar, watched it as it reached the top of its arc, saw Fleck's arms tense and his face grimace as he made to bring it down on her.

She shoved herself off the wall, hurtling towards Fleck like a human missile. She didn't know if the animalistic cry in her ears was from her, from Fleck, or just the roar of her mind. Either way she didn't care.

Her shoulder connected with the chest and chin of Robert Fleck, sending him stumbling backwards, the rebar useless now, released spinning in the air before thudding into the wall where Claire had been a second before.

Still Claire ran forward, her feet scrabbling on the floor, pushing the man backwards, Fleck's own legs scrambling desperately backwards as he began to stumble under her momentum and weight. They moved into the middle of the room, like an awful parody of a dancing couple before his legs gave way and they fell to the floor, Claire on top.

She drove her knee into his groin, hearing the satisfying grunt, then brought her elbow down, aiming for the bridge of his nose, but Fleck was able to twist his head away in time, so that it was her forearm that connected with his forehead instead.

His body thrashed beneath her, trying to buck her off him, but she used her knees to grip his torso and hold on, like a rodeo rider on a young untamed bull. She grabbed his head, avoiding the gnashing teeth, planning to pound it down onto the floor.

But then, she could no longer feel Robert Fleck beneath her. She could no longer see him, at least not the adult one. She was no longer in that derelict tenement block fighting for her life with a serial killer.

Instead she was in a child's bedroom. A Denver Broncos poster was on the wall. In the bed, covered by a thin, dirty, cheap looking blanket, lay a boy. His skin looked waxy, greasy. A sheen of sweat covered his features. His glassy eyes stared up to the ceiling where a bare lightbulb shone dimly.

The boy licked his dry lips with a dry tongue.

Then she saw there was someone else in the room. Another boy. Younger than the one in bed, but otherwise a carbon copy. She recognized him. She had seen him before. That time he had been in a hospital bed, dressed in blue and white stripey pjs, crying miserably.

This time he looked no less wretched. He sat at the side of the bed, staring at his older brother.

The boy in the bed seemed to come around slightly, he too suddenly realizing there was someone else in the room with him. His head which seemed too big for his neck and body swung round to look at the boy kneeling beside the bed.

He attempted a smile, but his dry lips wouldn't stretch.

"Just you now Robbie, my little soldier. Just you now."

Then Claire was back in the building fighting for her life with the crazed adult version of Robert Fleck. During the vision, her body had gone limp, and taking advantage of this sudden, unexpected opportunity, Fleck had grabbed it with both hands.

She came around as she was being flung off Fleck, landing on her back, once more the breath, so precious at that altitude, knocked from her body. Her head bounced off the floor, making her ears ring. Then Fleck was on top of her, his knees on her chest.

She saw his eyes dart to something to her left, then watched as he leaned over, her brain still confused from the vision, the bang to her head not helping her efforts to regain clarity.

Then she watched as he straightened up, a look of gloating triumph on his face, and her eyes went to what he held in his fist. She went cold when she realized what it was.

The knife he had held to Clint Goldmann's neck.

CHAPTER TWENTY THREE

A thin beam of light coming from a crack in the ceiling behind Robert Fleck reflected off the eight-inch knife clasped in his hand.

Dust motes swirled in the dank, chill air. A strange quiet had settled on the scene. Quiet but not silent. Both Claire King and Fleck were breathing hard. The exertions of first the chase and then the struggle had taken it out of them. When you were fighting for your life, it seemed to drain you more.

Claire knew that from experience. Your body called upon every resource available to it. Every muscle, every tendon and sinew.

But there would be a debt to pay. There always was. When the adrenaline had gone or had run out.

There were other sounds too. Somewhere in the distance a siren wailed, but any hopes or fears from Claire and Fleck respectively that it had come because of them, for them, were quickly extinguished, as it faded into the distance. No one knew where they were.

Then there were the sounds of the building itself. It creaked and groaned, as if it was shifting after a long sleep. The structure had been irrevocably weakened by the destruction that had already taken place. It was as if it had given up and longed to be turned completely to rubble.

Claire's eyes focused on the knife held above Fleck's head. Its serrated blade designed for slicing through steaks.

Somewhere in her mind, she worked out how long it would take for it to complete its arc, before it sliced through a different type of meat. That of her throat, or chest, depending on what Fleck's preference was.

Fleck's hand, the one not holding the knife was on her forehead, holding her head still. She felt his knees shift slightly on her, preparing for the strike, also preparing for her retaliation, perhaps expecting her to start bucking beneath him.

The two stared into each other's eyes. The madness she had seen before had gone. There was just anger, along with triumph. He may have been thwarted in his attempts to kill Clint Goldmann, but he had the woman who had stopped him, and that was almost as good.

Claire looked up at the man she knew was going to kill her. She knew whatever she did would not prevent the knife from coming down into her.

If she didn't die from the first blow, there would be others. Her hope was that it was instant, not a long lingering one, bleeding out on this deserted, dusty floor.

A strange calmness filled her.

She had faced death before. Many times.

She had even died. It held no fear for her anymore.

She had come to Denver to prevent the killing of any more people at the hands of this killer. Whatever happened to her now, Robert Fleck would not kill anyone else. She would be his last victim.

She did not want it, she would do anything to prevent it, but at that moment she was not scared by the prospect.

That alone gave her a power and a clarity that was new to her in these situations.

Previously when she had been so close to death, she had fought on instinct. Lashing out with everything and anything she could find, physically and mentally.

All of that understanding flashed though Claire's mind in a fraction of a second. Sitting on top of her, knees gripping her, one hand holding down her head, the other high above his own head sat Robert Fleck. He stared down into her dark eyes. Confusion starting to replace the triumph.

She didn't know if it was her complete calmness in what was so obviously a life and death situation that caused it, but the hand grasping the knife wavered.

Had he mistaken her serenity with an acceptance of death? Had whatever modicum of humanity that survived somewhere deep inside Robert Fleck found it harder to kill a prone target, someone who wasn't fighting to inflict the same damage on him, or was fighting tooth and nail for their own life?

Whatever the reason, Claire didn't care. All she knew was that Fleck's hesitation, his slight loosening of his grip on the knife's handle, the tiny slackening of his raised arm, all combined with the lack of downward pressure exerted by his knees had given her a straw to clutch onto.

And she grabbed it with both hands.

She drove the heel of her right hand into the Fleck's throat, then grabbed the forearm of the arm holding the knife with her left hand. Gripping it, forcing it back and away from her.

Fleck, shocked by the viper-like attack and choked from the blow to his windpipe, was forced backwards, his weight lifting off Claire's chest giving her extra leverage to force the knife further back away from her. She sat up, grabbing the arm with both hands now, the agonized groans and gagging coming from Fleck less than an inch from her ear, making part of her brain think he was trying to bite her.

She bent his arm, forcing the elbow the wrong way, producing an added level of anguished cries in her ear. She could feel his head thrashing about, banging into her own, but every ounce of her focus and strength was on getting the knife out of Fleck's hand.

She pushed the top of the arm back further, the pitch of the yelp in her ear going higher.

Then when she was sure she couldn't bend it any further, Fleck's grip on the knife loosened and it dropped to the floor with a clang. She continued to push, putting all her weight onto the figure sat on top of her, pushing him further and further back, feeling his balance shift. She also had an eye on the knife that had dropped behind them.

Fleck's body reached the tipping point and he fell back.

Claire allowed her body to fall with it, her left hand releasing the arm it had been gripping so tightly, and grasping for the knife. Both bodies hit the floor, Claire on top once more, a cloud of dust rising into the air. Claire's fingers crawled along the floor for the knife. They touched it; she felt the round smoothness of the handle.

A roar of rage erupted from Fleck beneath her, his body bucking, sending her toppling forward. She grabbed onto the cloth of his hoodie, but the hand touching the handle of the knife was shoved forward, sending the knife skittering into a dark corner of the room.

Fleck continued to throw his body into convulsions, like a fish thrown by a wave onto a beach. Claire couldn't hold on, and staggered to her feet. Her eyes searching for the knife, but the room was too dark, and she couldn't afford to turn her back on Fleck. Desperately she searched the floor for anything else she could use as a weapon, but the floor was remarkably clear of the rubble that had been strewn across every other surface of the building.

Two yards away, Fleck got to his knees, then stood up in a bent over crouch. He flexed his arm, the one Claire had bent back against its natural joint. His other hand rubbed his sore throat.

His eyes bored into Claire's.

The two looked at each other, neither sure anymore who was the hunter and who was the prey. Both were panting, both their bodies were battered and bruised. Both knew only one of them would win, *could* win this battle for survival.

Claire's mind raced, trying to see a way out of this situation.

Then her stomach leapt into her throat as she felt herself falling. With a terrible groan, the floor beneath her gave way, pitching her downwards to the hard concrete twenty feet below.

CHAPTER TWENTY FOUR

Claire's first thought was that she was having another vision.

As she felt gravity's irresistible grip pulling her through the floor, the structure finally giving way from the motion and movement from their struggle, she found herself looking for clues.

The debris from the ruptured floor cascaded down with her, around her and on top of her. A great tearing noise filled her ears, followed by the sound of metal, concrete and then two human bodies crashing to the ground on the floor below.

As Claire hit the floor of the story below, her legs buckled, pitching her to her right. That saved her life. A fraction of a second later a chunk of concrete, the size of the small refrigerator an ex used to keep in his office, just large enough to store an eight-pack of beer, plummeted down, hitting the hard stone floor and splintering into three.

She still did not come off unscathed. A group of the refrigerator-sized block's smaller siblings used her head and body as a crash mat.

She choked on the dust that was everywhere, pouring down from the broken ceiling and rising up from the floor below.

The noise became a trickle.

Claire couldn't breathe. She couldn't see. She couldn't move.

The blow to her head meant she was struggling to think straight, especially without the aid of those other senses. Her number one priority was to get air into her lungs. A task made almost impossible as every time she drew a breath in, it was accompanied by a handful of coarse dust and grit, reducing her to a coughing fit.

Gradually it dawned on her that this wasn't a vision. They were vivid, they were like experiencing the emotions through another individual, but she had never felt pain or actual physical discomfort in one.

This was life. Real life. And he knew that if she wasn't careful, it would be the end of that life, as a coughing fit somewhere behind her reminded her that she was in a fight to the death with a serial killer.

That gave her a jolt. Mentally her brain grasped for a crutch to help her to clear her mind, get back to fight or flight mode. And she knew the first of those was the only real option.

Physically, somehow her body managed to dredge up another surge of adrenaline, though the tank must have been way past when the warning light would have blinked on.

She managed to get her first air into her lungs without coughing. A small but important victory. Behind her the coughing had also ceased, and she could hear groans and the sound of rubble being lifted, moved.

It wasn't just a case of getting to her feet; she had to do it before Robert Fleck.

Claire managed to sit up, lumps of plaster and a ceiling tile sliding off her. That sent another cloud of dust into the air, but around her the dust was settling. Beams of light that shot in through various cracks and apertures in the building's ruined structure picked out dancing motes of dust, but the air had mostly cleared. Everything around her was white, including herself.

The act of sitting produced a rush of nausea, but thankfully she was able to force it down with her willpower. Her hand automatically went to her forehead and when she peered at the fingers they were smeared with a thick red paste, a mixture of blood and the thick dust. There may even have been lead in there too from Fleck's flask.

She staggered to her feet, whirling round in the same movement, facing her enemy.

He got up an instant before her. Blood trickled from his nose, and despite being covered in the white dust, otherwise he looked ok.

She blinked, her lids dragging grit across her eyes, but she didn't have time to attend to them. She needed every tool available to her.

The two, the FBI agent, and the serial killer looked at each other. Like two boxers, battered and bloodied after eleven brutal rounds sent out for the final three minutes.

Her head had almost cleared, but it was still not up to speed. Otherwise, she would have acted quicker, reacted in the way her training had embedded into her.

Fleck leapt down and to his right, picking up another rebar. Whether it was the same one he had attacked her with five minutes ago - was that only five minutes ago her dazed mind shouted out - she didn't know. Or care.

He hefted it in his dust encrusted hand, checking its weight. Bits of plaster dropping off his hoodie with every movement, revealing more of the red beneath.

Claire circled to her right, away from the weapon he held in his right hand. Her eyes on him, waiting for the telltale tensing of his muscles, the change of position of his head that would give away he was about to strike.

But she also needed to find a weapon of her own. She couldn't just avoid his strikes. No matter how good she was at evading his blows, eventually her defenses would fail, and the reinforced steel bar would hit her. Breaking her arm, her collar bone, her nose, or simply knocking her unconscious.

The area they had landed in was larger than the confined space they had fought in before, but they were still hemmed in by walls, making a twenty-foot by twenty-foot square arena for their contest. The floor though was littered with piles of rubble, making it treacherous to step backwards blindly.

The two continued to circle, Fleck using the time to get better control of his mind and his body, knowing that time was on his side. He lashed out, bringing the three-foot long bar swiping down towards Claire's head and neck.

She leaned back, stepping onto a half-brick and almost losing her balance. The bar wrought the air two inches from her nose.

A smile cracked Fleck's face. That, along with the white dust that caked his features and the red blood pouring from his nose made him look like a clown. Not the kind you found in children's circuses though. The ones that inhabited nightmares.

It took two seconds for Fleck to regain his composure after the strike. It took that long for him to get the weapon back under control.

Claire made a note. It wasn't long but it may just be long enough to launch a counterattack. Or get herself armed.

Fleck made a couple of feints, each one getting a reaction from Claire, which in turn made his smile grow wider.

Claire's mind desperately sifted through possibilities, her brain now working as well as she could have hoped. Her preliminary search of the ground around her had produced nothing she could use, other than a brick.

That would give her just one chance, and if it didn't work, she would be very vulnerable to a counterattack of Fleck's own. Those weren't odds she liked.

She flexed her shoulders, mentally assessing her arms, then leapt to her right as Fleck lunged forward wielding the bar like a medieval swordsman.

Fleck spun round, standing where Claire had been just a split second earlier. The smile still on his face despite his miss. He knew, like Claire, that time was on his side. She had to avoid him every single time. He only had to score one blow.

Claire's mind went back to a lecture she had attended as part of her training when she was still a young, green agent. It had been about the use of the mind, even in violent situations. The lecturer, a willowy woman with rigid gray hair, had tried to convince a skeptical audience that their minds were always their greatest weapon, but so also was the mind of their adversary.

Claire remembered walking out afterwards, listening to the mocking chatter of her mostly male colleagues, who were deriding the approach. Claire had not let their attitude put her off and had discussed the arguments the lecturer had brought up when she had next met Bernadette for a coffee.

She licked her lips, instantly regretting it, as her tongue brought back a crust of acrid dust.

In front of her Robert Fleck stopped, and started circling the other way, forcing Claire to do likewise, bringing the deadly rebar more and more into play.

Fleck gave a little nod, aware that the clock was ticking on this stubborn woman's ability to continue to survive against all of the odds.

She cleared her throat, not trusting her voice to speak, but knowing she would only have one chance.

"Just you now Robbie, my little soldier. Just you now," she said, trying to imitate as much as her vocal cords would allow, the voice of the young boy in the hospital bed.

The reaction was instantaneous and dramatic.

Robert Fleck stopped dead in his tracks. His face, even behind the mask of dust and blood seemed to crumple, his body sag. The rebar, held aloft, dipped as his grip slackened.

Claire had no time to see what he did next, because she launched herself at him, her elbow slamming into the killer's nose, sending him staggering back.

The confusion caused at hearing his dying brother's words, the words that had motivated and driven him onwards to get revenge, to get justice for him, was replaced by pain and anger. He let out a howl of rage as he felt his body fall, the second time in a few minutes he had been a victim of gravity.

Claire's hands grasped for the bar as the man in front of her retreated. The fingers of one hand, then the other gripped it, and with Fleck's mind concentrating on remaining upright she managed to wrench it from his grip.

She stood there, the steel bar held in front of her like a trophy. Fleck fell to the floor, fresh blood dripping from his nose, a look of disbelief written on his face, not understanding what had just happened, how this woman had turned the tables on him once again.

Claire stepped to the side next to the prostrate Fleck, away from his legs, the bar held in her hands.

"Turn over," she said, "lie on your front. NOW!" She emphasized the last command with a flex of her arms, leaving him in no doubt that if he didn't comply, the bar would find a home in his ribs.

Fleck looked up at her. For a second the two locked eyes, both testing, daring the other, then he turned around.

Claire stepped on Fleck's back, putting her weight onto him, pressing him into the cold concrete floor, extracting a gruff whine. Then she gently put the bar down, deftly getting the cuffs from her belt, and placing them on his dusty, bloody wrists.

***

The man opposite Claire and Wilson looked like a different person than the one they had found with a knife to Clint Goldmann's throat. To the one that Claire had fought with in the partly demolished building.

He looked smaller. Weaker. More frail.

The anger was gone. It was as if when that departed, so had much of his strength.

He sat at the table where he had just been read his rights, had his prints taken and a pair of overalls given to him, and wept. Great shuddering sobs wracked his body.

His face was more like the one Claire had seen in that vision, of Robert Fleck as a small, lonely, deeply sad young boy.

Despite being only too aware of what this man had done, the lives he had ended, others he had ruined - despite trying to kill her, Claire couldn't help but feel a twinge of sympathy for him.

His life had been set on a course by events out of his control when he was still too young to comprehend them.

The bitterness and anger had grown over the years, become uncontrollable. Deep down he thought he was doing it for the right reasons. What other ways were there to fight back, to get justice for boys like Robert Fleck. For men that boys like Robert Fleck ultimately grew into?

Then she thought of Josh, the little boy who because of Fleck would grow up without a mother and the glimmer of sympathy disappeared.

She watched him being led away, knowing that the city's troubles had not been solved by this one man's arrest, but happy in the knowledge that she and Wilson had at least played their part. That they had done what they had been brought to Denver to do.

She looked across at her partner. Wondered if the same thoughts were going through his head. Then her own thoughts turned to another matter, one that needed broaching, uncomfortable though it would be for them both.

There was no time like the present.

CHAPTER TWENTY FIVE

It wasn't the way she had expected the conversation to start.

Claire took a sip of her beer, licking the foam from her top lip. The bar was doing brisk business and seemed to cater to a mix of hipsters and businessmen and women from the nearby office blocks.

She had showered, changed, and patched up the cuts and grazes as much as she could. She felt better than she had when she had dragged Fleck out onto the sidewalk and flagged down a passing police car. Wilson had arrived on foot and panting two minutes later.

She felt better, but she still longed for a day when her body wasn't wracked with pain from one injury or another picked up in the line of duty.

It had been a hectic chain of events. She had been killed, brought back to life, burned, and now had fallen through a ceiling; all while being attacked by a serial killer armed with a knife then a reinforced steel bar, in a city that had descended into anarchy.

If it wasn't so painful, she may even have found it funny.

Wilson's questioning face at the high table opposite her brought her back to the present. Back to what he had just said to her.

"I want to help you, Claire. I *can* help you, I'm sure. You don't have to do all this on your own," he had said, as soon as he had put the two beers on the table. It had the sound and delivery of a speech he had rehearsed endlessly in his head, but that didn't make it any less welcome to hear.

"I mean about the visions," he said, obviously misinterpreting her silence, her hesitation.

She smiled, hoping it would show him that she was grateful. That she appreciated him reaching out, attempting at least to help her with something she knew only she could deal with.

"Thanks Mark. I genuinely am grateful, but…"

"…but you have to do this on your own?" he interrupted.

Despite herself she smiled again. Nodded. "Yeah," she said.

Then her face took on a serious look. "It's only because they only happen to me. I know you mean the best, but how can you help? How can anyone help? It's me they happen to. It's me who suddenly sees these terrible images, feels these horrible, raw emotions. One minute

I'm having a normal conversation; the next I'm whisked away into the mind of a sick killer."

She took another sip of her drink, aware her hand was shaking.

"No one can understand what that is like. No matter how hard they… you… try. No one. It… It scares me half to death Mark." She looked into Wilson's eyes, saw pain there, not for him but for her. A swell of emotion, of not quite desire, but a very real warmth for this man erupted inside her. She had just been more honest with him about what she was going through than she thought she could have been with anyone. More honest than she had been with herself.

"I know I won't properly understand, I know that, but surely knowing that I believe you, that I will always be there to talk them through with, to… to even cover for you if that's what you need or what you want… then surely that will help. In some small manner?" His voice was almost pleading.

She looked at him for several heartbeats before answering.

"Yes. Yes it would. Massively," she said, reaching out with her hand and placing it on top of his. "Thank you. You will never know how grateful I am." She took another sip, a longer one. "Sometimes I think I am going mad. That this is the first sign of my mind cracking up. I worry about what they are, why I am having them. What causes them, what it means about my brain, my mind."

"Then I worry about when I am going to have one. Will I be in the supermarket and suddenly be in the mind of a killer? What about if it happens when I'm driving, or…"

"…on a tightrope…" Wilson joked.

Claire laughed, glad and amazed that she was able to.

"Yes, on a tightrope."

"The doctor said there was no damage, didn't he? That he could see no damage to your brain?" Wilson asked.

"Yeah. Nothing he could detect anyway. But… this is so weird, maybe it wouldn't show up on any normal tests. I mean…" a look of astonishment lit up her face, "I am seeing things that happened in the past. Before I was born. I'm seeing things that are going to happen. How is that even possible? How would that show up on a regular MRI or CAT scan?"

An easy silence hung between them as they each pondered the question. The background buzz of the other patrons in the bar providing a soothing soundtrack.

"There is another side to this," Wilson said.

"And that is?"

"Well, without your visions, Robert Fleck would not be behind bars and Tyrone Conrad and Grant Holt would still be alive. There's no telling how many more innocent people they would have killed. How many people wouldn't be at home this very second, playing with their kids, speaking on the phone with their mom."

"Yes, I have thought of that too," Claire said. "But what does that say about our skills as detectives? That we have to rely on some strange out of body visions to solve cases?" She laughed.

"You know that isn't the case, Claire. You're the best detective I've ever seen. And as long as I'm on this earth you won't have to face anything you don't want to on your own."

They stared into each other's eyes, and Claire realized her hand was still on his.

Wilson was the first to break contact as he reluctantly looked at his watch.

"Come on," he said downing the rest of his beer, "we have a plane to catch."

She stood up, and finished her own beer, then tentatively touched her chest which was sore from the fight with Fleck. Or the fall. Or both, she grimly mused.

Claire watched as Wilson made his way to the door, opened it, and looked back smiling at her. She realized neither had mentioned anything about what she had said in the hotel bar the previous night. That neither of them had said what that meant going forward for their personal or professional relationship. At least not directly.

She smiled. She guessed that it no longer needed saying.

EPILOGUE

Home. Well, the precinct anyway, which to Claire felt more like home than anywhere else. That was something that as a thirty-two-year-old woman she really needed to address, but that was for the future. This morning there were more pressing matters to see to.

One of them needed fixing so she could move on with her life, and finally leave her old one behind. The other one, the one involving the Artist, that needed fixing or Claire – and countless other women and men – would have their life ripped from them by the most dangerous individual she had ever encountered.

"Agent King, welcome home."

Claire spun round in her chair to see the Chief standing behind her. She vaguely wondered if he too knew she felt more comfortable at her desk than in her empty apartment, but then decided it was merely a turn of phrase. The Chief wasn't known for his astute observations on his employees' home lives.

"Thanks, Chief. You weren't wrong. About it being a war zone. It was like dancing on a powder keg."

"Never took you for a dancer, agent," the flicker of a smile touched his lips. "Good work." His eyes went to the empty desk next to her. "I take it you didn't leave Agent Wilson in Denver?"

"No, Chief," Claire said, her own eyes resting on the empty chair, "he's on leave. A family matter."

The Chief's eyes stared at the empty chair for a couple of seconds as if he could bring the man back by the sheer force of his will, then he returned his attention to Claire.

"Keep me up to speed with what's happening with the Artist."

"Will do, Chief. More info has come in regarding that sighting. I'll be on it right away, and let you know what it means for the investigation. If anything."

"Do that." The Chief made to walk away then looked back at her, his eyes studying her.

"Have you changed your hair, agent?"

"Yes, Chief. Thought I could do with a change," she said, her thoughts going back to walking in the salon, whipping off her cap, and revealing the charred mess she had been left with after the fire at the Moynahan house.

The Chief looked at her for another couple of seconds, then nodded and walked off.

Claire watched him go, a smile stretched over her face. "Home sweet home," she muttered, then returned to her laptop. She had received a reply regarding the sighting of the Artist, but she needed to do something else first.

There had been another email that needed her attention that morning. Another email in reply to an information request she had sent. She had allowed her mother's case to take second fiddle for too long. Now she had committed to it; she fully intended to give it her full attention.

She opened the email.

There were several attachments. That took her by surprise. The assumption she had made was that very little had been done on the case. It had been processed, briefly investigated, then filed away. She realized that was the narrative her father had peddled all these years. That the death of his wife, and by association, he, had been ignored, forgotten about.

She opened the first attachment. It contained pages and pages of information. A quick look at the sizes of the other attachments showed they were even bigger.

She sat back, a puzzled look on her face.

This gave the lie to what her father had believed all these years. What *she* had believed. It also meant that looking into the case was going to be a whole lot more involved than she had thought.

She closed her eyes and thought. Despite her earlier resolution, there was no way she could shelve her other work while she waded through all of those files. It would take days. Weeks. Even then there was no promise that she would find anything. She would have to carry out her investigation into her mother's death in the background.

Her father wouldn't be happy, but when was that ever not the case? The most important thing was that she *was* investigating it.

She opened the other email.

There had been a reported sighting of the Artist a little over a week ago in West Virginia. She had sent an information request asking for more information. She would quickly be able to ascertain if it was genuine or not.

Her eyes greedily devoured the words on the screen. Her heart started to beat faster. She didn't know if it was with fear or because she felt the net was closing in on him.

After what had happened, the investigation into the Artist felt personal. He knew where she lived. They had stared into each other's eyes. Deep down she knew that he felt the same way about her.

She picked up the phone, dialed a number.

"Yes hi, this is Agent Claire King," she said. "I need to book a flight to Richmond, West Virginia."

NOW AVAILABLE!

ONCE HE FEELS
(A Claire King FBI Suspense Thriller—Book Four)

FBI Special Agent Claire King dies chasing a killer—and is resuscitated minutes later to realize she has changed. Dark images flash through her mind in a newfound power, visions leading her towards serial killers. A new serial killer strikes, mailing greeting cards to his victims before he kills them. With this ominous warning in hand, can Claire save the next victim before it's too late? Or can this killer be leading them astray?

"Molly Black has written a taut thriller that will keep you on the edge of your seat… I absolutely loved this book and can't wait to read the next book in the series!"
—Reader review for Girl One: Murder

Once He Feels is Book #4 of a long anticipated new series by critically-acclaimed and #1 bestselling mystery and suspense author Molly Black, whose books have received over 2,000 five-star reviews and ratings.

FBI Special Agent Claire King has a reputation for brilliance, for being able to crack serial killer cases that no other agent can. Before she died and came back to life, she relied solely on this brilliance. But now that she has this fleeting, newfound power, Claire is confused: should she follow what she knows? Or what she senses? Are visions more powerful than intellect?

Or will they lead her right into a killer's trap?

A page-turning and harrowing crime thriller featuring a brilliant and tortured FBI agent, the Claire King series is a riveting mystery, packed with non-stop action, suspense, twists and turns, revelations, and driven by a breakneck pace that will keep you flipping pages late into the night. Fans of Rachel Caine, Teresa Driscoll and Robert Dugoni are sure to fall in love.

Future books in the series are also available!

"I binge read this book. It hooked me in and didn't stop till the last few pages… I look forward to reading more!"
—Reader review for Found You

"I loved this book! Fast-paced plot, great characters and interesting insights into investigating cold cases. I can't wait to read the next book!"
—Reader review for Girl One: Murder

"Very good book… You will feel like you are right there looking for the kidnapper! I know I will be reading more in this series!"
—Reader review for Girl One: Murder

"This is a very well written book and holds your interest from page 1… Definitely looking forward to reading the next one in the series, and hopefully others as well!"
—Reader review for Girl One: Murder

"Wow, I cannot wait for the next in this series. Starts with a bang and just keeps going."
—Reader review for Girl One: Murder

"Well written book with a great plot, one that will keep you up at night. A page turner!"
—Reader review for Girl One: Murder

"A great suspense that keeps you reading… can't wait for the next in this series!"
—Reader review for Found You

"Sooo soo good! There are a few unforeseen twists… I binge read this like I binge watch Netflix. It just sucks you in."
—Reader review for Found You

Molly Black

Bestselling author Molly Black is author of the MAYA GRAY FBI suspense thriller series, comprising nine books (and counting); of the RYLIE WOLF FBI suspense thriller series, comprising six books; of the TAYLOR SAGE FBI suspense thriller series, comprising eight books; of the KATIE WINTER FBI suspense thriller series, comprising eleven books (and counting); of the RUBY HUNTER FBI suspense thriller series, comprising five books (and counting); of the CAITLIN DARE FBI suspense thriller series, comprising five books (and counting); of the REESE LINK mystery series, comprising five books (and counting); of the CLAIRE KING FBI suspense thriller series, comprising five books (and counting); and of the GRACE FORD FBI suspense thriller series, comprising five books (and counting).

An avid reader and lifelong fan of the mystery and thriller genres, Molly loves to hear from you, so please feel free to visit www.mollyblackauthor.com to learn more and stay in touch.

BOOKS BY MOLLY BLACK

GRACE FORD MYSTERY SERIES
NEARLY MINE (Book #1)
NEARLY SAFE (Book #2)
NEARLY FREE (Book #3)
NEARLY GONE (Book #4)
NEARLY HIS (Book #5)

CLAIRE KING MYSTERY SERIES
ONCE HE SEES (Book #1)
ONCE HE LONGS (Book #2)
ONCE HE TAKES (Book #3)
ONCE HE FEELS (Book #4)
ONCE HE KNOWS (Book #5)

MAYA GRAY MYSTERY SERIES
GIRL ONE: MURDER (Book #1)
GIRL TWO: TAKEN (Book #2)
GIRL THREE: TRAPPED (Book #3)
GIRL FOUR: LURED (Book #4)
GIRL FIVE: BOUND (Book #5)
GIRL SIX: FORSAKEN (Book #6)
GIRL SEVEN: CRAVED (Book #7)
GIRL EIGHT: HUNTED (Book #8)
GIRL NINE: GONE (Book #9)

RYLIE WOLF FBI SUSPENSE THRILLER
FOUND YOU (Book #1)
CAUGHT YOU (Book #2)
SEE YOU (Book #3)
WANT YOU (Book #4)
TAKE YOU (Book #5)
DARE YOU (Book #6)

TAYLOR SAGE FBI SUSPENSE THRILLER

DON'T LOOK (Book #1)
DON'T BREATHE (Book #2)
DON'T RUN (Book #3)
DON'T FLINCH (Book #4)
DON'T REMEMBER (Book #5)
DON'T TELL (Book #6)

KATIE WINTER FBI SUSPENSE THRILLER
SAVE ME (Book #1)
REACH ME (Book #2)
HIDE ME (Book #3)
BELIEVE ME (Book #4)
HELP ME (Book #5)
FORGET ME (Book #6)
HOLD ME (Book #7)
PROTECT ME (Book #8)
REMEMBER ME (Book #9)
CATCH ME (Book #10)
WATCH ME (Book #11)

RUBY HUNTER FBI SUSPENSE THRILLER
IF I RUN (Book #1)
IF I TELL (Book #2)
IF I LIVE (Book #3)
IF I FORGET (Book #4)
IF I RETURN (Book #5)

CAITLIN DARE FBI SUSPENSE THRILLER
COME GET ME (Book #1)
COME FIND ME (Book #2)
COME TAKE ME (Book #3)
COME CATCH ME (Book #4)
COME SAVE ME (Book #5)

REESE LINK MYSTERY
BEYOND REASON (Book #1)
BEYOND REACH (Book #2)
BEYOND REPAIR (Book #3)
BEYOND DOUBT (Book #4)
BEYOND NORMAL (Book #5)

Made in the USA
Monee, IL
26 May 2024

58973911R00085